Table of Contents

Fanchette's Pretty Little Foot

RESTIF DE LA BRETONNE

Translated By Richard Robinson

Sunny Lou Publishing Company
Portland, Oregon, USA
http://www.sunnyloupublishing.com

Translation: 2nd Edition, 28 November 2020
(from the original French edition of 1769).

ISBN: 978-1-7354776-1-9

Fanchette's Foot

or **The French Orphan Girl**
An Interesting & Moral Tale

A young Chinese girl putting her covered & clad foot forward will do more damage in Peking than the most beautiful girl in the world dancing naked at the foot of Taygete. – Complete Works, J.-J. Rousseau, Tome IV, p. 268.

Introduction

If my only purpose had been to please, the overall fabric of this work would have been different: Fanchette, her nanny, an uncle & his son, with a hypocrite, would have sufficed for intrigue; Fanchette's first lover would have been revealed as the uncle's son; the story's development would have been more natural, the denouement more striking & more lively: BUT IT WAS IMPORTANT TO TELL THE TRUTH.

To Madame L***, a Merchant's Wife

Madame,

While I am dedicating this work to you, it is to the Graces that I consecrate it. Born into a condition that is closest to happiness, you join virtues & talents to the seductive charm of a pretty face: cherished, adored by everyone around you, you are happy in the *feelings you inspire: they are not at all tyrannical like those of love; they do not have the coldness of respect; they are gentle & flattering like those of friendship. That is the precious advantage that the greats almost never enjoy: beautiful Madame L***, fortune has treated you more kindly than them. One honors them, but one loves you: what a difference!*

It is not, Madame, the case that I should want, like so many others, to lower the nobility of the blood, to consider every rank as equal, & equipping myself with a false indifference to fortune, insult its favorites from afar: no, I recognize all their advantages: I admit that they are great, & that they deserve one's envy. What a joy it is to serve efficaciously the State; to approach the Father of the Country; to lay claim to his trust sometimes; to offer a helping hand to the less fortunate among us, not in the manner of those who have limited means, but by assisting entire provinces! Surely, not all hearts enjoying so many glorious prerogatives are made of glass!

Do not however believe, Madame, that, in this respect even, heaven would have you less advantaged than them: in this enlightened century, merchants enjoy the general esteem: like the greats, they serve the Estates[1] & all humanity, but in a different manner: it is not at all by winning military victories, governing provinces, administrating justice or finances: it is by furnishing men with what is agreeable, useful, & necessary. What benefits their immense works do for society! They let their citizens enjoy the productions of two worlds, & bring the most distant of peoples

---

[1] Estates: the three estates, or social classes of society: the clergy (Church); the nobility; & the people, from the middle class (bourgeoisie) down to the lower class of peasants, poor, & homeless.

closer: it is the merchants who make previously bar-barous nations grow familiar with the commodities of life, & grow more refined gradually: it is because of them that they will become in turn a refuge for the arts & sciences: without them, agriculture, that first source of all our goods & property, would remain languishing & discouraged: from one end of the world to the other, obeyed like a monarch, without troops, without the frightening apparatuses of com-bat, their probity is the assurance of all their power.

Madame, in what way then can those who are distinguished by illustrious birth flatter themselves to have an upper hand on your condition? Ah! If there is any advantage, it is in you that I see it: what posses-sions are preferable to that sweet life that ease & af-fluence procures? One does not tremble before you; one treats you with consideration, & that suffices. For the majority of men, what is that so vaunted good fortune of being powerful, if not the sad prerogative of being able to appease dissolute desires, which a humbler fortune would have put the brakes to? Yes, MADAME, be proud of your station in life: it is useful & necessary: the dukes & lords have no nobler titles.

Fanchette, like you, MADAME, was born among that class of respectable citizens who apply themselves to commerce: her attractions, which make all hearts submit to her, you possess them too: deign to introduce her to high society: she could not appear under a more charming & virtuous guide.

I have the honor of being, with the most pro-found respect, MADAME, your very humble & very obedient servant,

– R. D. L. B.

Part One

Chapter I

A kind of preface.

Parturient montes, nascetur ridiculus mus.[2]

I am the veridical historian of the brilliant conquests of a beautiful young lady's pretty little foot. O you! astonishment & terror of the universe, celebrated conquerors, Ninus,[3] Sesostris,[4] Alexander the Great, Julius Caesar, Charlemagne, Genghis Khan, virtuous Henry IV, fiery Charles XII,[5] & you yourself, my country's hero, the immortal King Louis XIV, – lower your banners.[6] You have reigned over men; your redoubtable power makes them tremble; & Fanchette, young, without title, without noble birth, but with a seductive little face, eyes full of gentleness, & a foot... ah Heavens! a foot... as never before seen, it is so pretty, it reigns, through Love, over all hearts. Its triumph is much sweeter than what so many victories procure for you: to keep in check the subjects she has subdued, she needs only to make an appearance, *& take a step.* Just as formerly that famous

---

[2] *Parturient... mus:* Latin for "The mountains are in labor, a ridiculous mouse will be born."

[3] Ninus: mythical founder of Ninevah.

[4] Sesostris: legendary king of ancient Egypt.

[5] Charles XII: of Sweden.

[6] lower your banners: in other words, recognize your inferiority relative to the conquests made by Fanchette's foot.

Semiramis, by letting down his beautiful hair before a mutinied people & showing his naked breast, calmed the revolt of his enchanted, seditious rebels. Or rather: just as in our days one sees the lovely L***, clad in a cute slipper, attracting to her little foot a crowd of admirers' gazes: there is not a single young man who does not envy the lot of her lucky husband. If by a smile that beautiful lady encouraged those whom she has charmed, among the military, she'd be a Condé[7]; among the Poets, a Voltaire; among Prose writers, a Rousseau; among Musicians, a Rameau; among Painters, a Boucher; among all artists, great men; among all men, lovers.

What bombast; after such a run up, what else is there to say?... But, dear reader, you should know that it is common practice when one writes the stories of living people, or those whose families are influential, to use grand words & highfalutin phrases to express insignificant things. Moreover, my subject is not as tiny as might be imagined. The attention women pay these days to heighten the graces of a pretty little foot, & our experience in this domain, seems to tell us that it can instill passions without the need for any additional help. But what am I saying? Why limit myself to our century, & make conjectures, when history furnishes us loads of examples? The *radiance* of the beautiful Judith's shoe *dazzled Holofernes,* before *her beauty made a captive of the* Assyrian General's *soul.* The father of the ferocious Vitellius could not view the pretty foot of the Empress Messalina without being struck by strong emotion; *he obtained permission to remove her shoe, & took possession of one of her slippers, which he carried about with him*

―――――――――――
[7] Condé: the Princes of Condé, the cadet branch of the House of Bourbon.

everywhere he went, & which he often kissed. Could the reason for this be that, in women, in those charming creatures destined to please, nature wanted everything to be enchanting & seductive? It would seem so. These lovely female magicians turn everything they touch into a vanquishing talisman: everything becomes a dart shot by Venus' imp, Cupid, from the moment they touch it.

Chapter II

Most singular.

At four o'clock in the evening, a Thursday, I was crossing the rue *Montorgueil*, in order to walk down that of the *Comédie Italienne*.[8] They were putting on the twenty-fourth representation of *Moissonneurs*. A multitude of brilliant carriages, that barely touched the pavement they moved on, rolled with a fracas, splattered mud on good girls, men of talent, & the rest of that useful population, which (fortunately) one could not do without. Me, poor Heer, heir of Mézeray's cynicism (but not his avarice), muddied to the waist, I *took refuge* in the doorway of a fashion merchant's shop. My appearance, heteroclitely adorned, excited, in a bevy of girls who filled it, that inextinguishable laughter of the Gods of Homer. I turned my head, without ire (for I have the modesty of believing myself ridiculous-looking), – I wanted to see all those pretty girls laughing: my eyes fell on one, & only one, among them & my heart continues to flutter. They were dressing her. O God, how beautiful she was!

---

[8] Comédie Italienne: an opera house & theatre originally for Italian works by Italian players of *commedia dell'arte* companies.

Her hair, blacker than ebony, contrasted with the lily white color of her skin. Her coiffure gave her a little bit of a mischievous look; the alert & dark pupils of her eyes sparkled as with fire; her tender gaze tugged at men's heart strings: carnations & roses have less radiance than the color in her cheeks. One got a glimpse of two firm globes of dazzling whiteness, that her corset no longer constrained; a short skirt exposed the lower part of a leg... Heavens! What to compare it to? But, more seductive still than anything one could imagine, there was her foot, that pretty little foot, which would make so many heads turn; it was wearing a pink shoe, so well made, so worthy of enclosing so pretty a little foot, that my eyes, once fixed on that charming foot, could not turn away. "Beautiful foot!" I said softly to myself, "you do not walk on the rugs of Persia or Turkey; a brilliant equipage does not save you from the fatigue of having to bear up your masterpiece of a body full of graces; *you walk in person*: but you shall have a throne in my heart."

As I continued to think in this vein, the dreadful racket of carriages began to die down behind me; the streets became unencumbered, & I stood there unmoving. One of the companions of this pink-slippered beauty, nearly as pretty as she, & whom a charming young man caressed, fixed her attention on me: I heard her say: "Ah, Fanchette, look how he looks at you!" These words yanked me out of my revery; I exclaimed, with an enthusiasm that was more than poetic: "Yes, Fanchette, divine Fanchette; in the provinces, in the city, at court, in the street, neither queens, nor princesses, nor duchesses, nor marchionesses, nor the sumptuous wives of our heroes of finance, none of the ancient or modern beauties, present or future, none of them can hold a candle to you; they are nothing compared to you, & never will be."

After this escapade, I was about to walk away, when an old man of my acquaintance, whom I had lost track of for a long time, came up to me: he recognized me; I embraced him; he takes my hand; he leads; we enter the fashion merchant's shop; & the beautiful Fanchette welcomes him in the most flattering manner imaginable.

Chapter III

Which will not impose on the reader.

Kathégètes (that's the name of the old man) conversed for a long time with the charming girl, whose pretty little foot had so keenly caught my eye: their dialog seemed short to me. In the same way that, recently arrived from the provinces, a spectator becomes all eyes & all ears at the *Opera*: sometimes it is the decorations, at other times it is the instruments, the music, the machines; sometimes the actors, & above all the actresses; at other times the levity, graceful movements, voluptuous attitudes, those movements by the dancers that seem so natural, where all their art is hidden & the feelings seem nuanced; they occupy him, they transport him: finally, the spectacle ends, the curtain drops, but he continues to see it & to hear it; & me, ravished with admiration, I was standing there looking at Fanchette & her young companion, while the old man had already exited: when I realized this, I blushed & hurried out after him.

I wanted to put some questions to him; he stopped me cold. – "You," he said to me, "who feeds only on chimeras, you unhappy author of books, worse even, I want to procure for you the means to tell the truth for once in your life at least. Important business occupies me today. It has to do with bringing back to her lover, to her family, to the fatherland, a young person, whom vows made against her will were going to bury alive in a convent, & to marry my ward. In one week's time, pay me a visit; I have some memoirs; you will learn an astonishing story; just the facts... it will be quite the scandal."

"One week! That's quite a long time," I interrupted him, "for the impatience you have just stirred in me."

The old man was going to respond when his ward appeared; he left me & joined him. I will instruct my readers about this matter, & the incident that occasioned that delay.

The morning of the eighth day had scarcely broken when I rise from bed trembling with excitement. I fly to M. Kathégètes' house: he hasn't gotten out of bed yet; he is woken: I enter his room; he gets dressed; he looks for the manuscript, but does not find it; he calls a boy who serves him, a big lout, newly disembarked in the capital; he puts a question to him, to which the response was, for me, dear reader, like a knife stabbing me in the heart: this wretched boy had taken our story away to have curlpaper made out of it! We will have to write it ourselves, the old man & me. The chamber valet runs up; he still had some deplorable scraps of the work, cut into triangles, in hand. It is easy to imagine my disappointment, on reading them. Attempting to console me, the old man recounted for me the facts in broad terms. This only augmented my suffering: it was the story of the pretty Fanchette! But the hacked up details, would they be able to replace what had been lost? I had come to his house filled with highest hopes; I left it empty-handed, saddened, exhausted.

Two weeks passed: I had already forgotten by then that I had only recently been on the verge of wearing the glorious title of historian, & that I had been on the verge of becoming an equal to the Rs***, Fs***, Vs***, & above all Ts***, of illustrious past, whose heroes are more like each other than those I had to celebrate, when on entering a CAFÉ, where *virtus bellica gaudet*[9], I heard two young officers disputing rather heatedly about something, like two young bachelors from the Faculty of Medicine might argue about inoculation. I draw near: they were speaking about a manuscript. This word is interesting to an author. I pricked up my ears: one of them denied the authenticity of it, the other defended it: they pull me into the debate, & ask me to serve as arbiter; I ask (in imitation of lawyers) that I be given *a copy of the contentious document* & several days to form my opinion.

Dear reader, you can imagine my surprise, when casting my eyes on this manuscript, I recognized, from the very first lines, the story that that wretch of a chamber valet had cut to shreds! The story of Fanchette's foot! The good-for-nothing lout had understood my regrets & those of the old man; it gave him an idea: he was clever enough to take hold of what he had shown us, & which we didn't put

---

[9] *virtus bellica gaudet*: Latin for "military virtue rejoices," or "military virtue finds enjoyment." Presumably the café was frequented by military men.

much stock in, hid the pages that were still intact, scrambled to find all those he had made into curlpapers, uncurled them, put the whole back together as best he could, & had a copy made of it. With the manuscript thus reconstituted, more or less, he went to sell it to the Abbot ***, who, it is widely known, buys all sorts of works, which he has the effrontery to publish as if he were the author of. According to method, this famous writer had disfigured this manuscript, under the pretext of correcting it, so as to make it unrecognizable. A dandy entered as he was finishing up.

"Another work?" he asked, with a mocking tone of voice.

"Um... um... it's a small thing."

"Let me see it... may I see it, my dear man?"

"Yes, this note here...."

"My faith! The author is good!"

There is nothing more foolish & more ignorant in the world than a dandy. After reading it all, the dandy notices the struck matter, all which was in the abbot's handwriting. Certain rumors floating about in public augmented his suspicions; the end of this note that he had just read, & others that were crossed out, confirmed them: he seizes the occasion of a visit he was about to make next, takes possession of the manuscript, runs to show it in order to ruin his friend's reputation: more unfaithful still, he makes a new copy of it, corrected, mutilated, augmented this time, in order to make it even more different than what the novelist had come up with. He loaned this copy to a woman of vapors[10], who read it from cover to cover without yawning, found it deliciously written, & nevertheless struck out, restituted, embellished additional passages of it, & left the refined manuscript sitting on her dressing table, where the officer found it. This latter person handed it to me, as I have just said; I made him understand my rights, which he didn't dispute. And it is in this way that, by a trick of fate, the work came into the hands of its legitimate proprietor. Lucky for the public & myself, & old Kathégètes as well if death hadn't prevented him from seeing it again!

End of the prefatory material.

Chapter IV

Which ought to be the first,
Wherein one becomes acquainted with Fanchette.

A wealthy fabric merchant in the capital, named Florangis, inhabiting rues Saint-Denis or Saint-Honoré (little does it matters to us) had a vast boutique where one could discover nothing but four walls; in recompense, at the back of it was a large staircase, that twenty people could ascend at the same time without rubbing elbows. At the top of this beautiful staircase was a dark shop, whose window casings, provisioned with shutters, permitted only a feeble light to enter. All the fabric, as well by our manufacturers as by

---

[10] a woman of vapors: either a prostitute here, or a woman of certain social class who had, or was supposed to have, suffered from a "case of the vapors" (fainting spells, etc.) occasionally, & at the right time, which at one time was considered to make a woman seem more feminine.

those of England & India, could be found there; one had only to pick & choose. In addition to this beautiful shop, that large boutique, & that commodious staircase, this merchant had a wife, pretty as an Irish peasant,[11] coquettish like a working girl,[12] a lover of the game, the gambling table & ***. [13]

Despite possessing the means & potential to secure him a fortune, the merchant's business, which one has just read about, went to ruin; but before it did, his wife had a daughter. For several years, one believed that the girl would grow up to be rich, & her education was in line with that false idea. Fanchette (that's her name) was twelve years old when she lost her mother, who could not survive the family's disaster, which she had caused. At fifteen, she suffered another, even greater, blow: her father, a good, honest, hard-working man, but who could not, like so many others, stand up to his wife, fell ill: he could see that his end was near; & his daughter, whom he was leaving behind at an age of passions & seduction, made him weep bitter tears. He called her to his bedside, moistened her with his tears, gave her a talk both heartfelt & wise, which one will read in the next chapter.

---

[11] Original footnote: Abbot *Prévôt* says that these are the most beautiful women of Europe.

[12] Original footnote: A great man (M. de Voltaire) has just come out with a small work (*The Princess of Babylon*) in which he proves that one can apply this phrase to the girls of the *Opera*.

[13] Original footnote: The woman of vapors maliciously left a big gap in this place, which the scholars of future races will not fail to fill in with nonsense.

Chapter V

Instructions given opportunely.

"Dear child, what will become of you when your father is gone! If I were leaving a fortune to you like the one I had received from my parents, I would still be afraid of your being seduced, although it would have been easier for me to find a safe place for you to live; but I leave to you, my daughter, for your inheritance, nothing but my poverty, & your beauty, two sources of distraction & crime... O Fanchette! It is only for you that I wanted to keep living, since I lost the woman I loved... too much perhaps; but who, through a look or by a smile, always filled my heart with love & tranquility again. All-powerful God, as I have said in all my prayers, allow me to raise my daughter, that I might be her guide until I deliver her unto the arms of the spouse You destine for her! Heaven will not permit it: as of today perhaps it will end a career. Alas! it was a long & happy one. Praise be to You, great God! For the advantages I have enjoyed; keep faraway, I entreat You, keep faraway from my dear child, – the misfortunes of her mother & those that I have suffered....

"Fanchette! Cherished daughter, listen to the dying words of a father: you are beautiful, you are poor, you are innocent: remember your beauty, & be ever on your guard against seducers; you will see them, my dear child, at your heels; do not grow proud of your charms, for fear that they might make you vile & guilty. Oh! If you knew with what contempt a rich man looks down on a girl without means, after he has seduced her! If only I could instill this idea in you as I feel it! How terrible a woman must feel once she's consented to have her favors ravished by a haughty tyrant, who looks down on her in her defeat with an insolent & disdainful air! My daughter, modesty & innocence are tender flowers that a breeze can bruise, that a touch can tarnish, that an imprudence can irreparably destroy. Remember this, my daughter, about your innocence, that treasure you possess, to have a clear idea of its inestimable value, & to tremble at the least danger that threatens it by the faintest touch. Don't let your poverty bring down your soul; keep, O my dear Fanchette, that noble pride, which sees the height of debasement in disorder, & not in indigence: be modest; keep your feelings in line with your fortune: those amusing arts that you learned, forget them; those talents seem designed to give a new luster to virtue, as well as to beauty; but from today forward don't let them occupy any more than a second place in your mind; a lucrative employment, & whose emoluments might meet your needs, that's the essential thing for you now: you have no other source than that, my dear daughter, by which to quench your hunger or your thirst without incurring dishonor. Look on, dear Fanchette, ah! look always on those elegant women with horror, whom crime weighs down with their jewels, trinkets, profane headbands & ribbons, destined to decorate victims immolated in debauchery: those unfortunate women haven't one single diamond, not one jewel, that does not advertise their being up for sale, & that debases them even in the eyes of libertines; they spend an ignominious life in what appears to be pleasure, but is in fact a real calamity. Tell me, my daughter, do you think she is happy who no matter where she turns up excites whispers of indignation from among sensible people, biting epigrams from dandies, & disdain from those of her own sex? What a fate! And that is only a small part of the anguish she feels, & perhaps the lightest. Ah, my daughter! all the riches in the world will never be able to redeem her honor!

"Alas, my dear child! Heaven has taken everything away from us... Your mother had a brother; for a long time he was my first, & my best, friend: my ruin brought on his own. He collected together what little remained of what fell out, & quit his fatherland, taking his wife & a son in the cradle with him, to try his fortune in some other hemisphere. Either his misfortune, which we caused, embittered him, or death took him, – we never discovered what became of him. If however he is alive, & if one day he should return, you would discover in him another father. But maybe at that time you will be without a safe place to live. O misfortune! what follows your acts are even crueler than you are; you destroy the very bands that bind societies & families together; you throw a man, after the tempest, onto deserted & savage shores, or nobody recognizes him when he returns. Dear Fanchette! Heaven will protect you, doubtless... He changed his name from Rosin, to acquire a new line of credit: that's all I learned by chance; but what name he took, I don't know. My daughter, take this precious gift; misfortune could not oblige me to remove the diamonds that embellished it: it is the portrait of your mother. Keep it with this letter, which she drew up for her brother, when she was on her dying breath. If he hates us, he will be unable to resist the display of tender feelings that this letter contains; if he still loves us, you will be all the dearer to him: guard carefully these precious gifts, the last presents from a father who loves you....

"Of my many friends who overwhelmed me with testimonies of their affection in those most happy days before our tragedy, only one man remains, who shows an interest in you. Although excessively rich, he lives a simple life. I know of only one fault he has: it is having too much of that meticulous devotion, that loads him down with practices, good perhaps, but far from being essential or necessary, & fills his time which could be better spent: aside from that, people ascribe to him the title of an honest man. It is into his hands that I will commit you, O you! dear child, the only possession of mine whose loss makes tears fall down my cheeks at this moment. Obey him, my Fanchette, as if he were me, this new father, to whom I commend you, while I am dying."

The good merchant stopped there: Fanchette burst out into tears: she covered her father's hands with kisses; while he said to her in a soft voice broken by sobs:

"My daughter, promise me that I will remain in your heart; that my lessons to you will guide you & your conduct, &..."

"Dear father!" the girl cried out impetuously: "Ah! what kind of a person do you take me for, as if I could remain insensible to your kindnesses! My father!... never... no never, your dear name, your advice, your tender feelings for me, they will never leave my memory, nor my heart...."

The moribund's eyes grew animated; a smile of satisfaction appeared to trace itself across his hideous & emaciated face; his paternal heart beat: he owed the happiness of his last breath to his daughter.

"Bless her, O God!" he said in a quiet voice: "My God! bless her, this dear child, the most precious gift ever; for she has given freely of her sweetness to me on this my dying day." These last bursts of emotion were too strong & too sweet for him; his debilitated organs, his battered body, could not sustain them: a feebleness overcame Florangis; then the man he had just spoken about to his daughter entered the room. He administered some assistance to his unfortunate friend, who, on re-opening his faded eyes, recognized him, & showed signs of joy.

"Fanchette," he added, in a trembling voice, "here... is the man... who wants... to act as your father...."

And on saying this, spoken with great effort, he closed his eyes; nothing more could be heard from him save sighs & wheezes, powerless activities of nature that continued to struggle against destruction. Fanchette was pried away from her father's body, which she was pouring over with her tears: the eyes of her father's friend (the girl noticed) remained dry.

Chapter VI

Misleading appearances.

"Beautiful Fanchette, calm down, calm your grief, it is too keen; these sighs & these sobs will not bring your father back to life; I will show you the same feelings your father had; my efforts, my thoughtfulness to see not only to your needs, but to your desires, will exceed all he could have done for you. My only desire is to see you happy; count on me; you are the absolute mistress of my house & my person." It was in this way that M. *Apatéon* expressed himself, in order to console Fanchette, eight days after her father's death.

He followed up his words by actions: the young Florangis girl was dressed in the same sort of elegance that she had worn in her younger years; before he died, her father had been giving her only coarse fabric to wear, on account of his limited resources. But in eight days' time, she reappeared in her former magnificence: in addition to her mourning attire, she wore jewels, a wristwatch studded with diamonds, material made with a discriminating taste, – the most seemly & modern styles of clothing & dress. In spite of her fickleness due to age, these beautiful articles could not efface from Fanchette's heart the memory of a father who had cherished her, & they could not weaken in any way her feelings of regret for his recent passing. But she was not ungrateful to M. Apatéon either; she was permeated with respect for him; but she sometimes said to herself: "Ah! If only I had all this from my parents instead; if it was my virtuous father who accompanied me this evening on the promenade, how happy I'd be!" And the girl wept. I do not pretend to deny that a small leaven of pride contributed to the maturing of these regrets, perhaps they were also due to some tender feelings; but pride is a virtue, if it elevates the soul, & shows us the servility by which to receive, when it is impossible for us to act in the same manner.

Every day M. Apatéon procured new amusements for his ward: he passed entire days alongside her. Music, instruments, dance, the promenade, shows, the theater, & fine suppers succeeded one another. Honestly, Fanchette saw no other men than her teachers; it was with M. Apatéon that she danced. The adorable girl was quite far from enjoying herself; she was experiencing a style of life from which tumult & spontaneity were banished, & where innocent pleasures only varied. Everyone in the house lowered their eyes in her presence, & they spoke to her with nothing but respect. M. Apatéon dined face to face with her; but as soon as he left the table, Fanchette was free. "Heaven be thanked," said the young Florangis girl sometimes, "for this friend of my father, for his not having abandoned me! How worthy he is of my respect, my esteem, & my gratitude!"

Rising in the morning, that is to say at ten o'clock, M. Apatéon, refreshed by a long & peaceful slumber, asked whether his ward was dressed; she didn't keep him waiting; they exited the house together & went off to a temple of worship, where the devout person set an example of fervent piety. Then he brought Fanchette back home: they ate lunch together; the dance teachers & music teachers arrived: after her lessons, they sat down to dinner; after which they took a long walk in the garden that was almost as delicious as *Eden*, until vespers, which they went to hear among the religious: the weather was beautiful, the Tuileries, the Luxembourg Gardens, the Boulevards, were, for one hour, Fanchette's theatre of triumphs: after which, they went to the show or the theater, or they returned home.

I have forgotten to paint a picture of M. Apatéon. He was a small man, about fifty years old; neither handsome nor ugly; of larger than average portliness; with a fresh & florid taint; with soft, benign eyes that look down at one's feet; discriminating without appearing so; a lover of ease & luxury, & a good meal; always maintaining, when conversing, an air of good-naturedness which won people's hearts. He was on cloud nine when, during their public promenades, he heard men praise Fanchette from head to foot; he let his gaze fall stealthily at his ward's pretty little foot; & by distraction, he said out loud: "How charming it is!" He took particular care in ornamenting that part of the young Fanchette's body with the most elegant footwear: he was always busy trying to find a buckle for her shoes that was gallant enough & of fine enough taste; after having visited unsuccessfully but successively all the jewelry shops in town, he ended up designing a new form of shoe himself, that all Paris admired: because when it came to the finery & attire of the gentler sex, M. Apatéon knew better than anyone else in the world what was needed. He was said in his youth to have invented the short cape, to hide a small defect in the waist of a pretty mistress, whom he was crazy about: calashes, on another occasion, were another emanation of his brain: he had trailing dresses brought to the pretty Nic***, after she had touched his heart, because that belle, although pretty in the face, didn't have so fine a leg; & for Fanchette, he always prescribed that her dresses be made a little on the short side, so that nothing might hide her pretty little foot.

Chapter VII

A danger one could have predicted

Young, innocent, & virtuous Fanchette lived in calm & tranquility with her benefactor Apatéon. Often she noticed that when she was speaking with him, he turned red in the face, as he pressed her hands: sometimes, as if without thinking, he finished drinking what she had left in her glass on the table: when they returned home together, instead of giving her his hand to help her down from the carriage, he took her in his arms, & carried her to the stairway: on ascending, her feet barely touched the ground, the obliging old man lifted her up, & carried her breathless to the door of her apartment: under the pretext that too close-fitting a shoe might injure her, as soon as they were inside he presented to Fanchette a pair of elegant slippers; then he fell to his knees, before her feet, to prevent her from having to bend over, & he removed her pretty shoes. The girl was touched in her heart with a true feeling of gratitude for all his efforts & attentions: sometimes, however, they made her blush; but she considered her feelings of immodesty as the beginning of ingratitude; & she felt horrified.

One day, when the weather was very hot outside, the old man had his affairs to attend to: Fanchette stayed home alone, in her apartment, & began reading *The Entertaining & Moral Letters of C****. This reading put her to sleep: she was lying on the sofa, with one of her feet resting on a chair, & the other having dropped down onto the parquet. One could see the beginning of her leg, & in particular that pretty little foot, a work of art, a gift of grace; it was in plain sight. The good M. Apatéon comes home again, & flies to where all his desires converge. He enters her apartment by a secret door, into the beautiful Florangis' room. He sees his ward sound asleep. The smarmy old man's heart beat with a violence: he drew near to her, quivering with delight; he got down on his knees; he kissed that charming foot a thousand times. He didn't want to stop there: the leg of this adorable girl was tempting him; but the movement of his heavy mass on the floorboards woke Fanchette up. She sees him, his mouth glued to her slipper: she lifts herself up, blushing. The old man, kneeling & thrown into confusion, immediately took a different tack, & letting out a heavy sigh, he directed his eyes languishingly up to look at a sacred image that was before him: "Great Saint," he exclaimed with warmth, "watch over this lovely girl, whose feet I have just kissed in humility; that her beautiful soul might be inundated with the graces that give salvation, as her body has all those graces that give rise to admiration. Praised be the Creator, who made her so charming... & so wise!" And on saying these last words, he gets up, & he kisses passionately Fanchette's hand, who withdraws it sharply.

"I love you in God, my dear child," said Apatéon alarmed. "We are not like those atheists, who have only illicit intentions when loving; have no fear of a man who adores in you no other way than the Creator himself." Then he sat himself down beside his ward, who understood nothing of his actions or his words; he took her two beautiful hands from time to time into his own & pressed them; sometimes he slipped his arm around her svelte & slender waist, taking a mental measurement of it; he hazarded even to steal a kiss. Fanchette, unsuspecting, was suffering however; she no longer felt her heart expanding for him: previously she rejoiced in M. Apatéon's presence; presently she wished him faraway from her. She thought all this; but she betrayed none of it. Apatéon thought his triumph easy: but he didn't dare risk anything just yet; he put off to the following night the execution of a plan that he had formulated from the moment Fanchette was under his control.

Chapter VIII

Fortunately!

At supper, the sensual Apatéon wanted her served with a meal that was even more refined than usual: he also wanted to engage her in drinking, following his example, some of those delicious beverages that warm the blood & put impetuous desires in the heart.

"My dear girl," the devout man said, "all these things here are made for the Elect; they don't corrupt them; on the contrary, they sanctify them."

But Fanchette knew nothing about sanctifying debauchery; she had learned from her father to love sobriety. She associated, according to custom, the Naiads with Bacchus. The old man could not convince her. That day then, he didn't retire immediately after escorting her to her room; he wanted to help her get undressed. Fanchette was quite innocent; but a natural light of reason guides the fairer sex in rules of decorum: the girl felt she had to put an end to her complaisance with regards to M. Apatéon; she would never have consented; the old man was *obliged* to make her cede.

Once alone, Fanchette wished to reflect; but before her was an impenetrable chaos to untangle; from the bottom of her heart, she felt feelings of fear: for the first time, that door that led from her apartment to his, & which had often reassured her in the night against a thousand infantile fears, gave her a feeling of anxiety. She went to find the Lady Néné, M. Apatéon's sexagenarian housekeeper. It is worth mentioning that Lady Néné, the daughter of Fanchette's mother's wet nurse, had always loved Fanchette's father, the merchant, dearly, & her affection carried over to his daughter. M. Apatéon's ward begged Lady Néné to sleep in her room.

"Why, Mademoiselle?"

"I'm afraid."

"You're afraid! Eh! Of what?"

"I don't know."

"I can see that, but no matter; whatever pleases you; I agree."

"My lady?"

"Yes?"

"You will come?"

"Yes."

"Really?"

"I promise."

"My lady?..."

"You're crying, Mademoiselle? My dear girl, what's going on?"

"Woe is me! I've lost my parents. My father, he's no longer here!"

"The poor child! She's breaking my heart! Calm now, calm, my sweet girl: Monsieur has only kindness for you, & as for me..."

"Ah! My lady!"

"How's that! Would it stop?"

"No, but..."

"But?"

"He's not my father!"

"Sweet little girl! She misses what she's lost! You need to accept your situation, my dear girl."

"I'd rather... M. Apatéon had less kindness for me."

"You surprise me, Mademoiselle, what kind of language is that!"

"He confuses me. For example, I don't know why, when he carries me in his arms, when he kisses my hand, I feel distress... a distress I cannot compare to anything. A poor orphan girl like me cannot, without shame, help thinking that he renders services she would not accept from a domestic except with repugnance."

The old housekeeper knitted her brows, & gave her all her attention now. She made her explain what services she was talking about, & her astonishment redoubled.

Now, Lady Néné knew about men; but the edifying exterior of her master had always impressed her. She accompanied Fanchette to her room, & climbed into a little bed, which she had moved next to the young person's. Both of them spoke in whispers.

"I feel better now," said the amiable Florangis. "This afternoon he surprised me; I had fallen asleep; he was kissing my foot when I awoke...."

"Really! really! The foot! Yours! He knows all about them... But how is it you didn't hear him come in? Your door is stiff & makes noise."

"He didn't come in from there."

"Ah! By where then, if not by the door?"

"By the one that leads to his room."

"What do you mean?"

"I thought you knew about it."

"A door from his room into yours?!... that's the first I've heard of it."

"Nothing truer however; & tomorrow, if you want, I will show you."

They heard a noise, & stopped talking. For a long time, they remained silent: finally sleep sprinkled its magic dust on the young Florangis, & the old woman dozed off, when Apatéon, who had no inkling of his ward's arrangement, slipped into the room from his apartment. He approached with caution, & held his breath; he touched the bed; he could tell it was occupied; a thousand times his errant & perfidious hands advanced to want to violate the sacred trust that a friend, on his his deathbed, had confided to him in good faith; & a thousand times the fear, not of crime, but of failing, held him back. Finally, he hears a sigh; he cannot contain himself any longer; his mouth searches for Fanchette's mouth; his hands push & prod...

"O, Heavens!" he cries out, recoiling in horror; "What have I touched! That is not my pretty Fanchette, it's a monster in her stead!"

The old woman, who had just woken up, muttered something to herself in a raucous voice between her teeth, which put the dirty old satyr to flight.

"My girl," said the housekeeper, waking Fanchette, "I know too much; good thing I was here at least!"

Chapter IX

By chance.

"Who would have guessed it!" said the old house-keeper to herself, while dressing herself in the morning. "I have been working for M. Apatéon for twenty years now: I was forty years old when I started, & nevertheless he has never said an improper word to me, & never touched me in a way that offended my modesty, except last night... How men change! & it takes very little to sink a virtue that, maybe, the rudest trials have not yet rocked! O! he doesn't know who he's dealing with. The good M. Florangis was quite correct in his thinking: alas! He knew that even our best friends deceive us. But look at M. Apatéon for a moment, with his sweet little face! He needs a sixteen-year-old girl, with a complexion of lilies & roses, a great looking body, good-looking legs, & the prettiest little foot that one could ever imagine in France! He will not touch her if I can help it!"

While thinking like this to herself, the old woman was finally dressed, & Fanchette awoke.

"Nanny," said the young Florangis, "you said last night you knew too much?"

"Eh, well, Mademoiselle, I was mistaken: what I wanted to say was that I knew enough."

"But, that's the same thing. What do you know? Tell me."

"What do I know? I know that, to put your mind at rest, it is absolutely necessary that I sleep here each night; & that, during the day, it would not be a bad idea for you to keep your door open."

"Ah! My good lady! Then you see very

clearly that what I'm feeling is not vain terrors & the little fears of children? Also, it's not that I'm afraid, but it's an anxiety, a... I don't know what, nanny, when M. Apatéon is near me."

"Darling child! He's your father come back to life. Come on now, Mademoiselle Fanchette, I love you a hundred times more than ever. O! You... Look at this, I'm crying. But it's for joy." Ah! she thought to herself, if only all those young girls with saucy faces didn't resemble her! We wouldn't see so many good-for-nothing men & shameless sluts! Then: "I'm going to go & prepare Monsieur's lunch; he needs things that gratify a sensual voracity & provoke an unnatural appetite. Don't get used to it, my dear girl, that excessive consideration of his because it will not last forever. And if he speaks to you in a certain tone, if he mutters nonsense to you... when he takes your hand & wants to cheer himself up; stop him in his tracks, take back your hand, & look at him with anger: for clearly he is trying to test you. Good day, Mademoiselle; don't forget what I'm telling you, & you can always count on me."

The housekeeper, running to the kitchen, said: "He'll get what's coming to him, on my word! That faithless, wily, dirty old man!"

Fanchette reflected. It is impossible to express how entertaining it would be to read inside the mind of an innocent, virtuous, but above all ignorant sixteen-year-old girl: everything her imagination gives rise to resembles fairy tales; she puts her trust in everything; & nonetheless her fears make her see monsters everywhere; at the drop of a hat, they all dissipate, & her serenity is restored without cause, just as she faints without reason. For all that, indecisive & timid, she trembled for a long time before daring to hazard a step: she wasn't however defiant by nature; she was defiant only after having been fooled; she usually thinks only good thoughts about everyone she sees; & if sometimes she suspects nasty fellows to exist, she supposes them almost always among those she does not know. Yes, men notice nothing about a young woman except, when looking at her attractions, the most feeble half of what should affect them; she would become much more interesting to them if they could read her heart & discover there these treasures of innocence, frankness, lovable candor. But this happy age in life of hers passes quickly: surrounded by traitors & perfidious men, her young soul picks up vices, & arrives sometimes just out of adolescence at that point of depravity when she does not believe virtue to be necessary even; & there you have the work of men... What am I saying! Ah, pardon! I'm not at all one of those atrabilious misanthropes who look for nothing more than to denigrate the human species: no, I was momentarily confused; men, my fellow man, whom I cherish, whom I revere, are not capable of trying to destroy virtue in their loving, their charming, their divine companions! That's the work of libertines, those "agreeable" men who bring their inutility & corruption with them everywhere they go; those puppets, successors of the *Gauls*, no less unhinged, & more dangerous; those old men, who, with gold in hand, drag their disgust & libertinage behind them; & all those miserable men unworthy of the name human.

Fanchette's mind was led astray in a labyrinth of meaningless ideas: to pull herself out of this disturbing situation, she drew near to her harpsichord & played the most touching tunes on it. When a person is feeling melancholic, when she has thought a great deal, her soul is full & it searches for a way to open up. Fanchette accompanied the instrument with her voice; she let her heart dictate, & her songs exuded nothing but grief: the name of her parents got mixed up in them; her tears rolled down her beautiful cheeks as she pronounced their names while singing.

The beautiful Florangis was charmed by this pastime; a little nothing amuses a girl: Fanchette forgot the universe; & M. Apatéon, filled with the thought of his ward's nascent charms, quite a bit disquieted however by what he had felt the night before, got up out of bed. When his toilette was complete, he visited Fanchette in her rooms; he watched her for a long time before interrupting her. She was wearing only a negligee: her waist had never been so well delineated; she was wearing a pair of shoes white as snow, trimmed with silver braid; her pretty little foot kept the beat, & every movement she made, brought new desires into M. Apatéon's soul. He was beside himself, when he approached her; he took her into his arms & wished to ravish her with a kiss. The girl turned her face; the old man planted his kiss on the most beautiful hair in the world, & thought he hadn't lost much thereby. The fire of passion circulated impetuously through his veins. He lifts Fanchette off her seat, carries her to a wing chair; the adorable Florangis has no idea what he intends to do; but she defends herself as if experience had instructed her. Apatéon, an old hand at this, lets her defend herself for a bit; gains a strategic position, then another; finally, the innocent orphan, frantic, hardly able to breathe, & trying in vain to call out for help, was maybe about to suffer a tragedy, which she would have never been able to get over, when the housekeeper ran into M.

Apatéon's room to let him know that his lunch was ready & was running the greatest risk of getting cold. She couldn't find him in his apartment; she looked for the secret door, found it, & sees the infamous Tartuffe[14] all over his timid prey. Prudent woman that she is, she goes out the way she came in; runs, faster than she's run in thirty years, to Fanchette's other door, & raps on it forcefully.

She was just in time. Apatéon, nearly the victor, fears he will be discovered; he abandons Fanchette; warns her to keep it a secret "or else," & dashes for the secret door. The girl, worn out & soaking wet, cried out to enter.

"What's wrong, Mademoiselle?" said Néné.

"Alas!" responded Fanchette, crying.

"My dear girl," took up again the old woman, "tell me... explain to me... what happened?"

"I cannot tell you what M. Apatéon wanted from me; he tormented me. He wanted, nanny... I have no doubt about it; he is not what he appears to be. I'm too embarrassed to tell you what he wanted."

"What is it he wanted?"

"If you hadn't knocked on the door..."

"Ah! my dear girl! And as it turns out, I only stopped by by chance."

---

[14] Tartuffe: the main character of a play of the same name by Molière. He was the epitome of hypocrisy.

Chapter X

An unexpected resource.

They ate lunch. Apatéon kept his eyes lowered; in-genuous, Fanchette soon put him at ease. This lovable girl was far from guessing what her tutor had in mind. Her only thought was that he had wanted to do something indecent; he failed; she was satisfied; & she made a promise to herself to distrust any similar attempts in the future. Apatéon (who, like the reader, had believed Fanchette's knowledge to be more extensive), seeing her act normally, conceived new hopes, stoked by his hypocrisy & her cheerfulness.

But the governess, who, during the night, had learned much too much, who in the morning had found out even more, fortunately had all the experience that the young Florangis lacked. She saw clearly that sooner or later her master would triumph over Fanchette's innocence; she had first-hand knowledge, more than once, that by braving danger, one succumbs to it; by consequence, she resolved to get a good girl, over whom she had more authority than one thinks, out of that place.

It is very natural that my reader has no idea, as I have not told him, that Fanchette's father, on his deathbed, did not so completely trust his friend M. Apatéon that he didn't take precautions to protect his dear daughter from a seducer's traps, should they materialize. At the same time, he knew that Apatéon's housekeeper had dearly loved his wife; he knew her sense of honor: in consequence, he had entrusted to her a sum of money, what remained of all he had saved from financial disaster; what he could acquire from some of Madame Florangis' jewelry & clothing; his own even, which he had sold, as soon as he was sure that he had no more hope to live: the total came to about two thousand *ecus*. By a codicil, which was supposed to remain a secret, he entrusted the house-keeper with using that sum of money to place the girl with a woman employer, unbeknownst to M. Apatéon, if his good will should grow cold, or if for other reasons, which he didn't express & which had actually happened, her hand should be forced. The same document said that if Fanchette's uncle should show up one day, he would assume over his niece all the rights entrusted to others.

They returned from Church; they sang, danced, dined; they were going to go to vespers: the good Néné adroitly whispered into Fanchette's ear that she should feign the need for rest because of an indisposition. The girl didn't know how to feign; she told M. Apatéon quite plainly to go out by himself that day because she didn't want to accompany him. The old man insisted on the necessity of going to ves-pers; she begged him to desist; he was complaisant: he gave up & left.

As soon as her governess learned that Fanchette was left alone, she ran to her apartment, & without losing an instant in pointless speech, she handed her that document to read, which contained M. Florangis' last testament. The darling girl read it sobbing, & gave it back to Néné, who put it carefully away in the box she kept it in.

"So! Mademoiselle, would you have the cour-age now to put on again the clothes you wore when you arrived here; that sad proof of your misfortune, & leave the easy life you enjoy under the roof of a sub-orner!"

"A suborner!"

"Yes, Mademoiselle; the man who received you from your father's hands; for whom you ought to be a most sacred treasure, he deserves that name you have just seen in the document from your father: he wishes to dishonor & discredit you: to undo you. There is only one way to escape. Your good father! Oh! imagine the grief he'd feel now, – he had foreseen it. What do you say?"

"I say that I must obey my father. Ah, nanny! I have no interest in anything anymore! Nobody will look after me now! If M. Apatéon wants to do me in, everyone will want to do me in."

"Dear Florangis! I'm only a poor woman; but one day you will know my zeal; I love you so much... my dear girl, I will do the impossible for you. Don't waste time; leave these trinkets & the jewelry; they are, for a poor girl, sad signs, advertising either that she's up for sale, or the infamous price she's already paid perhaps for her innocence: put on your old clothes: here they are; I have just retrieved them; in order to go & speak with the most honest fashion merchant in Paris, a woman, whom you will enter into apprenticeship with; while I place with a notary the sum your father entrusted to me: Mademoiselle, all the Apatéons in the world cannot prevent an indigent woman, subject, among other things, to a thousand defects, from finding her happiness in being useful to you."

"Are you going to act like my mother then?" said Fanchette with a caressing tone of voice.

"Ah! Beautiful Florangis, one day you will not doubt that I have such feelings for you. By a stroke of good luck, my dear child," added Néné, "the merchant woman, although not a relative of yours, has the same family name. This makes you special in her mind, before she has even laid eyes on you; & to avoid all questions about your family, your connections, she will pass you off as her niece."

As they spoke, Fanchette found herself dressed in the modest clothes that Apatéon had made her slip out of when she first arrived, & she looked no less beautiful; they had become tighter & shorter; but what difference did that make? She didn't owe anybody anything for them: the adorable girl was content. They departed through a garden gate, without having been seen by the house domestics: Néné introduces Fanchette to the fashion merchant, says hardly a word, & hurries back. She arrived just before the devout Apatéon came home again.

Chapter XI

He will come again.

"Come, Mademoiselle," said the merchant woman to Fanchette; "You must not stay in the boutique, where someone might see you: my daughter will keep you company, & you will do your work with her in the room I plan to give you." As she spoke, the young Agathe gets up & runs, with a joyous air, to take the hand of the adorable Florangis. The governess had told the merchant woman everything, & her ward became a most precious treasure to this honest woman.

Agathe was a touching, blond-haired girl, tender, sincere; but lively, vivacious: she was only fourteen years old. At first sight, Fanchette charmed her: she took a lively interest in her, which was succeeded by a constant friendship, & they were ever inseparable. Fanchette made, under the guidance of her young friend, rapid progress at her work: she found a decided pleasure in it; one always learns quickly what one loves to do. For her own part, the good governess tried to procure for her all the amusements that were in her power. As I have said, she had deposited the two thousand ecus, that Fanchette's father had entrusted her with; she added to this sum what she had amassed herself for over forty years: the total amounted to a fund of eight hundred *livres* of rent; she had also put aside the wherewithal to pay for Fanchette's apprenticeship, & for her upkeep during the three years it needed to last, so that the young person would always have several years of revenue in reserve: at sixty years old, one is thrifty & provident. Néné gave her a harpsichord as a gift, & the books she asked for; in a word, she had promised to act like a mother to her, & she kept her word.

"My dear Fanchette," she said to her one day, "my family lived in poverty, but everyone, before me, has paid their tribute to nature; you are the person now who ought to interest me the most; accept these trinkets I give you, like tokens of friendship; they demean nobody."

Oh! How I love this nanny Néné! She was a laborer's daughter: during her youth, she came to the city, & served. She brought with her from the village her pudor, a tender heart, an appetizing figure, & a great deal of good faith: a boutique employee, a public prosecutor's clerk, a chamber valet, a maître d', &c., all deceived her, each in their turn, promising to marry her & never keeping their word: she enjoyed pleasure, but she always had a horror of crime; she became wise at the school of hard knocks. By the time the fire of youthful passions had been extinguished in her, she could relax: "Happy tranquility," she told herself, "how long it has taken you! Why weren't you the companion of my youth, as well as my old age!" Her heart was not however any less sensible: she loved Madame Florangis, & subsequently Fanchette, as much as she was able to love any person. Eh! Who can measure the feelings in a tender soul! But the girl was a real treasure to her: "Help her steer clear," she counseled herself, "of the heartbreaks I ran aground on, when I found myself the dupe to perfidy: let her experience deeply the inexpressible sweetness of always having been virtuous: alas! I cannot hide it from myself now; I was never able to be happy with any man but the first lover I favored; I would have turned red in the face in front of others."

This simple, ignorant woman, knew where to focus her acts of kindness; she could have spread her insufficient gifts thinly among a hundred orphans, & not made a single one of them happy: instead, she attached herself to Fanchette, & one will see what resulted from it. O you! whose well-intentioned & generous soul is moved to help the indigent, keep in mind the lesson of Néné's conduct; adopt a poor family; help a single one, if your fortune does not allow you to help more than that: any other manner of giving alms is vicious: you can instill mores in the family that you help; you will only make begging vagabonds out of those you give mediocre assistance to, to the effect that they depend on you only.

Fanchette rarely went down to the boutique: she still wore a veil over her face so that no one could recognize her. One day she appeared for a moment, to show her work to the merchant woman: she was wearing a calash which covered her head; but her short dress exposed the lower part of her fine leg & pretty little foot. A young man, in full mourning, entered with his governor, to make some purchases; his eyes were immediately fixed on Fanchette; her loosened waist, that leg, & that foot in particular struck him. He tried his utmost to see her face: the amiable Florangis noticed; she hastened to ask her mistress' advice, & then returned quickly to her room with Agathe. The grace of her step succeeded in enchanting the young man.

"Ah! she is so good-looking, Madame," he said to the merchant woman.

"That's merely conjecture, Monsieur," she responded.

"One cannot be ugly with... no, Madame, a woman with so much grace is never ugly. So pretty a foot can support only a beautiful woman."

That's not exactly true; but this young man had already started to fall in love, & one must not try to find exactitude & moderation in a lover's expressions. He continued to ask questions, to which the merchant lady (who never engaged in idle chatter with anyone, period) didn't respond except by monosyllables. His governor made a purchase, paid, exited; his ward appeared to follow him, but grudgingly; & Fanchette, back in her room, said to the young Agathe: "My friend, do you know that young man? Apparently this is where he shops? Will he return?"

Chapter XII

New conquest: will one be happy?

"Fanchette has disappeared! Nobody saw her leaving! Nobody knows what's become of her!... Ah, wicked people! You will give her back to me! But, may lightning strike me if... Somebody must help me find her, or, I swear... Fanchette! She was so cute, so well-behaved, so.... I'm about to lose my mind, if someone doesn't bring her back to me. A suitor perhaps has made off with her! & me, what a fool I am! For six months now I've been sighing... Sheesh, I should have brought it to a head. It would have been so sweet to hold her in my arms... I was planning on it: I was mistaken. Ah, I have to find her again! Pretty, delicate Fanchette, what mortal now savors kisses from your pink lips, kisses... ah! all the luxury I am surrounded with in life & wallow in are worth nothing to one single kiss of hers! She could not have left on her own initiative; someone took her from me; my domestics are part of the plot. Hola! Traitors! It will be death! If you don't confess to the truth, I will have you all hanged by the neck. How modest she was! But where was Néné then! When her pretty fingers struck the keys of that harpsichord; when her seductive foot kept the beat; when her so sweet, so touching voice sang out, I... I should have nibbled on her a thousand times. Cursed lunch! If it wasn't for you... Imbecile that I am! I could have consoled myself today at least: another man would not have plucked, from under my nose, the rose I've been nurturing, nourishing, watching over for so long. Ah!..."

It was in this way that M. Apatéon expressed himself after he had become aware of Fanchette's escape; after he had scolded Néné, whom however he didn't dare ask questions about regarding his vision of the previous night; after he had sent all his people out, into the country, to find & catch his pretty prey: & whose monologue finished by a furious yell. All the measures he took for a long time were fruitless: a poor woman, a girl, had gotten the better of him, a Tartuffe!

Fanchette was living happily & tranquilly: from day one, she had forgotten the abundance & the fine living; from the first instant, the jewels, the adjustments, cruel idols for which so many woman sacrifice their honor & their mores, didn't cost her a sigh. Her father's advice was traced in her memory: "I work," she told herself; "I fulfill the designs of the dear author of my days: Heaven will bless me." And Heaven blessed her.

The merchant woman had a nephew, named *Dolsans*, a young man of much promise; a disciple of *Michelangelo*, *Raphael* & *Lebrun*; an imitator of *Vanloo* & *Vernet*. He had just returned from Rome: on the first visit he paid his aunt, he saw the beautiful Florangis. It was a feast day: Fanchette was wearing a new dress, not very expensive, but extremely fetching; it was a gift from the good Néné: the beauty of her hair was heightened by a tasteful curling: a pretty bonnet seemed to have been placed on her head by the Graces' hands themselves, that is to say by herself, under Agathe's direction. A green pair of shoes, ornamented with a golden flower, wrapped her pretty feet. She was seated, her back turned, reading *Emile*,[15] when the young Dolsans entered. The first object that caught his eye was Fanchette's pretty little foot, posed on a small stool. His heart thumped. While embracing his aunt, he looked at her; while responding

---

[15] *Emile*: presumably by Jean-Jacques Rousseau.

to all her questions, he looked at her.

"What interesting things did you see in Rome?"

"Lots of things, aunt."

"A little more detail."

"Ah! What I find is seductive!"

"You painters, you are so enthralled with that city, you act as if it were a mistress: everything seems marvelous to you there: my faith, I've never seen your Rome; but Paris is just as seductive as she is."

"Aunt!..."

"Yes, my dear nephew, don't get upset: I will take the side of Paris against all the Romans."

"It's a marvel!..."

"A marvel as long as it pleases you. It has its Saint Peter's Basilica, as far as I've heard; but Paris has its Louvre & the Tuileries: connoisseurs have assured me that no edifice in the world would equal the Louvre, if it were completed."

"I'm not talking about buildings, aunt."

"As for the masterpieces of painting, one sees in the salon..."

"Oh, my God! I'm not talking about paintings either."

"The nation's character, the habits of its people? Ah! As far as that goes, my nephew, the entire universe should bow down before our country. What *amenities*, what elegance among our own! I see people of high-society, my dear Dolsans; I hear what people of substance say, that our present urbanity will serve as a model to all future races."

"I grant you all that, aunt, I will go even farther, if needed: Paris contains the marvels that surpass everything I've ever seen."

"Now you're being reasonable. We will soon have your works; clearly you will soon have become perfect? You don't say anything!" (He was drawing near, to get a better look at Fanchette, who had still not turned around.)

"Sometimes I embellish nature; but what I have just now seen is designed to make a man despair, or to make the ablest artist on earth outdo himself."

"Nephew," the merchant woman took up again, speaking into his ear; "stop right where you are: you know me: in spite of the feelings I have for you, an imprudence on your part would banish you from my home."

Dolsans understood what she meant by that; he lowered his eyes: after a moment, he lifted them just enough to see Fanchette's foot, & in his heart he said: "Ah!, If she were as ugly as she appears beautiful to me, the inexpressible charm of her foot alone would make me adore her."

Several of Fanchette's companions came in: her reading was interrupted: she got up: Dolsans, forbidden, immobile, watched her; he became intoxicated by the pleasure he found looking at her. With each step, the beautiful Florangis unleashed new charms; everything became beautiful under her feet. She walked in the same manner as the divine Cyprian walks, preceded by burning desires, accompanied by the Graces, & followed by the Pleasures. Dolsans wanted to pay her a compliment; but he found nothing that could express what he felt. He kept silent; his eyes alone did the speaking; & Fanchette maybe understood only too much of that language.

Young & touching Beauties, all conquests flatter your heart, which is still a novice; you see your triumph only: but a trap is hidden beneath the flowers, & behind the hedgerow; too often alas! There are those who would excite nothing but bitter tears.

Chapter XIII

There is one too many.

Pardon me, Mademoiselle, if I dare write to you before having introduced myself: but I'm completely unable to control my impatience; the occasions to see you arise so seldom that it's impossible for me to wait for them. I have barely seen you; you were as if veiled: the desire I exhibited to read my destiny in your eyes served only to deprive me rather of the pleasure that your presence gave me; & nonetheless I feel that my heart is yours forever. I am not so unjust as to complain of your flight; it only makes you more worthy in my eyes of the gift that I intend to make of my faith, my feelings, & my entire being. Yes, I swear by the holy Author of nature, that I would have no other spouse than you. I am rich, & I am overjoyed since I fell in love with you; before this, I never thought about marriage; I'm not born of an illustrious family; my family made its for-

tune in finance; I'm even more overjoyed: our conditions in life are the same, & the imaginary distance of rank, all the more tyrannical as it is less real, will not come between us.

I confess that your gracefulness alone has touched me; I have no idea if you are as beautiful as all the rest of you presages. Yes, Mademoiselle, I have no idea what it is that makes me shiver on seeing you. You have a shapely body: but it is not your waist: you have beautiful hands; your rounded arms are white as milk; your legs... it is not even that that has charmed me: my eyes have fixed themselves on the prettiest foot I have ever seen; I cannot stop looking at it, & my heart beats with a certain violence. To complete the enchantment, you spoke: God! What a seductive voice! No, no, it is impossible that with that touching of a voice you do not possess a fund of inalterable sweetness, innocence, candor in your soul; you have what it takes: whatever is necessary to make a husband happy... Ah, Mademoiselle! If you consent to be the reason for my happiness, believe me that I will not neglect to do the same for you. A man esteemed for his mores, who offers himself as a groom, ought not to be disdained: his intentions are pure; he offers the most precious gift to a girl, at the same time that he asks in return for the possession of that which sets the price of everything else, a kind & virtuous companion. Reflect on what I permit myself to write to you today: I have no more parents; for a short time still I am in the charge of a tutor; when I turn twenty, I will be my own master: such was my father's will: I can give you an exact date then as to when I will keep my promise. Accept the promise I make to you today that I am all yours. *I will do whatever it takes to know my destiny & your response.*

I am, Mademoiselle, with an attachment that will never waver,

Your, &c., DE LUSSANVILLE

It was in this way that he wrote to Fanchette, the young man who had only caught a glimpse of her, & who was obliged to leave, when his governor exited the boutique. This letter was delivered, by a lackey, to the merchant woman, who gave it to the young Florangis, telling her: "My girl, see here what someone has written to you; if it's what I suspect, I hope that you will do nothing without consulting with me & with Madame Néné first. Fanchette broke the seal, opened the letter, & read: the look on her face came alive, revealing the emotion in her heart.

"Here, Madame," said the girl after finishing it, handing it to her. The merchant woman was touched by the trust the young Florangis placed in her; she read it in turn.

"Fanchette," she picked up the conversation again, "what do you think of all this?"

"That men employ, to deceive us, ever more novel stratagems; that I must not respond to this young man, & I should avoid him."

"Beautiful Florangis! How delighted I am to hear you think so! However, my dear child, if this was a serious proposition, you shouldn't spoil it for any fault of his. This young man is kind: did you not find him so?"

"He would not be so dangerous if he had seemed less worthy of pleasing."

"You would be charmed then if he was speaking the truth?"

"Yes, Madame: but I'm almost sure he is a deceiver." (She was sincere at least.)

"My child, will you do whatever I counsel you to do?"

"Yes, provided my nanny is in agreement with you."

"She will agree to everything; I can assure you." And the merchant woman left Fanchette, who said to her dear Agathe:

"It seems to me, my good friend, that my heart is taken by this young man, in spite of myself: I hear a secret voice that tells me he is sincere, tender, & that he'll make me happy. That I would enjoy owing him everything!"

The fashion merchant considered the young Florangis as worthy of her nephew: "An honest girl, & so wise," she told herself often, would make Dolsans the happiest married man: she is not rich; but she is virtuous, modest; she will be economical & organized in her management of the home; that's quite a nice dowry in itself. When a girl adds beauty to wisdom & gentleness, she has more than what a noble birth & riches have to offer: her attractions hold the heart of her spouse, her gentleness captures him, & her conduct makes her family prosper."

And that is how common folk reason: among their superiors, it's something else altogether: those virtues that the good merchant woman esteemed so highly have become too plebeian: & it's in this way that everything in the world has its strengths & its weaknesses: Ah! If felicity, virtue, talents did not take their revenge on mediocrity, then the century's powerful people would enjoy too enviable a destiny.

M. Apatéon's housekeeper rarely came to visit. She was afraid of being observed. The merchant woman had barely left the room, when Néné entered. The touching Florangis was delighted to see her; her heart desired it: Lussanville's letter had moved her; she found pleasure in re-reading it; she had just embraced her nanny & was going to show it to her when Dolsans appeared: his aunt herself brought him in.

That pure joy, that smile of satisfaction, that timid blush, that delicious agitation, which the sight of a loved one causes, – one saw all this painted on Dolsans' face. Fanchette lowered her eyes. Emboldened by his aunt, encouraged by the presence of the good Néné, who knew him, the young man spoke: he paid the young Florangis the most flattering compliments; never had he shown so much wit, & he had never expressed himself with such ease: love made his conversation touching; his desire to inspire lent an air of truth to everything he said: it reminded the housekeeper of her younger years: she desired so perfect a spouse for her dear girl. She & the merchant woman left them alone in the room for a moment. Agathe even, whom Fanchette wanted to stay, followed her mother & the nanny out.

"My beautiful demoiselle," said the young painter, falling to his knees, "you see before you a lover who adores you; an unbounded joy, or a super-abundance of misfortune, that's what awaits me with your response. If you could flatter me with the hope of touching your heart one day; there is no one in the world besides you whom I desire: if you cast me aside, I will be the most lamentable of mortals: what might I expect?"

Fanchette turned red in the face. She sought, according to her habit, from the bottom of her heart, the response that she should give him, when someone knocked: Dolsans rose, the door opened, & Lussanville, the young, the adorable Lussanville appeared.

Chapter XIV

Wherein everyone is happy, for no good reason.

"If I had imagined, Mademoiselle, that chance would procure for me today the joy of seeing you, I would not have written; I come to beg your pardon for my temerity. Will I obtain it? The feelings I expressed in my letter, dictated by honor & by love, will they excuse me? To prove to you how sincere I am, I consent to stop speaking with you until their execution. Allow me only to present myself before you from time to time, either at temples of worship, or on promenades; & deign to tell me if I might hope to see my constancy rewarded one day! It would be unfair of me to ask you to explain yourself; I feel it: Well! Allow me only to interpret your silence. Two years is quite a long time to wait; but if the impatience I should feel is shared, how happy I would be! You say nothing... I will depart then; & this security, which I leave with you as a token of my sincerity, will prove..."

"I cannot accept it, Monsieur," interrupted Fanchette. And at that very moment, her nanny & the merchant woman came back into the room.

Their surprise was inordinate, on seeing the young man, who, without giving them any time to recover, repeats what he had just said to the beautiful Florangis, places in the hands of the governess an extremely valuable box, kisses his mistress' hand, upsets something on a chest of drawers, & disappears like a bolt of lightning, before Néné can think to refuse his present, or at least give it back again.

Dolsans couldn't tell if what he had just seen & heard was a dream or reality.

"Fanchette," said her nanny, "how is it that this young man knows you?"

The merchant woman explained everything. The young Florangis gave her the letter, which she read with astonishment: the governess opens Lussanville's box without further ado; on top was a promise of marriage duly signed, then a ring, an exceptionally handsome diamond, earrings, a necklace, & all the rest of it jewelry, all carefully chosen & more beautiful than the jewels that Apatéon himself had given her. It was no longer possible to return any of it, given nobody knew where the young man hung out or lived. The merchant woman grew anxious; Dolsans appeared desperate; Fanchette reflected; her nanny made up her mind.

"Oh, boy," Néné said to herself; "so what do we know: Fanchette is beautiful enough to inspire a lasting passion: this young man will soon be his own master; he is rich: what's more, he will make a name for himself: my dear girl will have a rank worthy of her deserts: what glory for her! What joy for me! What disappointment for M. Apatéon!... But alas! Men are such deceivers! Hadn't they all promised me as much? Fine! And wasn't I like just Fanchette, young, well-bred, wise?..."

For her own part, the merchant woman said to herself: "My nephew can find a richer one, just as virtuous, & who won't waffle."

And Dolsans: "The entire universe will never offer me again a girl so touching & so beautiful."

"Well, well! My dear Fanchette," said her nanny, "a choice needs to be made here that only you can make: neither Madame, nor I, should speak for or against either of these two men."

"That's exactly my same sentiment," interrupted the merchant woman.

"Decide for yourself," spoke up again Néné; "You must follow your heart: your lovers are both equally nice; they both appear guided by honor: what do you say?"

"Nanny," responded Fanchette, "You are like my mother; I will obey you. However..."

"Say it."

"Why oblige me, being so young still, to make a decision that will affect my future happiness? Wait until reason guides me; the light of its flame is still feeble in me & flickers: an imprudent inclination could decide for me, a foolish fire or false brilliance could deceive me, & set me up for eternal regrets."

Everyone agreed that Fanchette was right.

Dolsans himself approved from the bottom of his heart. He put a lot of stock in his efforts, in his aunt's protection, & even more so in his love. The nanny, the merchant woman, & Dolsans all left the room. The first of them, overjoyed, carried away with her the box of jewels, which the kind Florangis had asked her to take charge of; the nanny knew perfectly well which of the two lovers she preferred; & the young man hung on to hope.

Dolsans looked twenty-four years old. He was dark-haired, tall; his eyes had something overly active about them; his gait was easy: he had good-looking hands, & he held himself well. His physiognomy was spiritual; his fine & penetrating attitude humbled those who drew near him; his conversation was amusing & florid: he knew a lot & appeared to pride himself on it a little, although he affected to be of modest bearing. His character leaned towards tenderness; but his sojourn in Italy had made him jealous & defiant.

Lussanville, on the other hand, younger, more handsome, richer, & no less tender, was made to love & be loved in return. One could see frankness & candor painted on his face; his face had male traits; his look was noble & gentle; his long, chestnut-colored hair fell down below his waist; he had an aquiline nose; a delectable & vermillion-colored mouth; his complexion was delicate; his legs were slender & well-made. His soul was large & generous; honor & love alone held sway over it: he always kept his word: he was a faithful friend, a respectful & submissive lover, sometimes miserable, but always faithful.

Chapter XV

Wherein Fanchette interrogates her heart.

"O my father! Never has your daughter had a greater need for your guidance & feelings! Alas! Whereas yesterday my worthy father would have chosen a husband for me, today he is no longer... Unfortunate children, who lose their parents, ah! what unhappiness is in store for you! Without a guide, without friends, you will go astray; you will not find a generous hand worthy of leading you. Despised, debased, that's not the bottom rung of misery for you: if you have some beauty, wicked men will cast criminal glances at you; they adorn you to immolate you & to dishonor the ashes of your virtuous & dear parents. Oh! what sorrow if your parents were sad witnesses to it! But eternal night hides your ignominy from them, & the tomb becomes a refuge for them. And that is precisely what would have been my lot, if I didn't have that poor woman, born into servility, who passes her days in servitude! O Heaven! O God, who have been a father to me! What favors don't I owe you! Do not permit me, great God! to ever fail to respect that good old woman whom you gave me as a mother: whoever she choses, he will be my husband.

"If both of them, equally perfidious, sought to deceive me!.. but why would Lussanville be a seducer? He will stop visiting me until the moment I see proof of the oaths he just renewed... How my heart was moved when he entered the room! I felt an inexpressible satisfaction when I heard his voice. He didn't force me to respond. With what skill he spoke when faced with my silence!... And his gifts?... He didn't give them to me as M. Apatéon did; he doesn't require that I adorn myself for him; that... he wishes only to see me, without touching me, in places where innocence & modesty have nothing to be ashmed of. How tenderly he spoke! Ah! my father, doubtless, would have loved him; he would have given him his daughter's hand in marriage. And why then does my heart grow troubled merely at the thought of him? Why does it flutter? Can it be I love him? Is this what one calls love? I don't think so, but I would like to love him, & that he might always be faithful to me... he will not: a thousand other beautiful women, more beautiful than I, will seduce him; clever girls will steal his heart. He will forget me: I will be so upset!

"Dolsans... he cannot be as sensitive as Lussanville. Kind Lussanville! Dulsans says he loves me; and if he loved me with all his heart – if Lussanville forgot me, – would I still be happy? My heart is silent. Ah, Lussanville! Be faithful! But if he was not? I feel... I think... that I would be miserable. Poor orphan girl, abandoned, or rather, obliged to flee as from a monster, the only friend my father had left: it sits well with me to prefer the more lovable, the richer, who perhaps... who knows! is the more treacherous. O Dolsans! The logical choice at least is you, & my heart never despised its counsel. Irresoluteness that my father's wise counsel would have put an end to, you torment me for such a long time still! Heaven! help me to recognize the more worthy man between them, &, if possible, let it be Lussanville!"

Agathe came back into the room. Deeply buried in her thoughts, Fanchette forgot that she had promised to accompany the merchant woman & her daughter on a visit: the presence of her young companion jolted her memory: she gets herself ready, & wants to put on the pretty green shoes that Dolsans had seen: she looks for them, finds nothing, does not think too much about it, & exits with Agathe.

Chapter XVI

Wherein Fanchette's foot makes everyone bow down before her.

After the joy of seeing & speaking with the woman one loves, there is nothing so sweet as receiving from her hand the very image of her attractions: if this solace *in absentia* still lacks anything, the strongly smitten lover would see his mistress again in what made up part of her toilette; a piece of her attire re-calls all the charms he adores in her. What she touches is meaningless in itself, but for her lover, she has consecrated it, it becomes a treasure in his eyes.

And when swearing an oath to his beautiful mistress that he would love her forever, Lussanville had noticed on a chest of drawers her pretty pair of shoes; on exiting, he adroitly grabbed them; on rising from bed the next morning, he wrote this note:

BILLET

From the young LUSSANVILLE *to Mlle.* FANCHETTE.

I adore you; & to prove it to you, I con-demn myself to the cruelest punishment a lover could have: to be absent; but yesterday I stole the ornament of your pretty foot, which was the first of your attractions that caught my eye: it is not that I need some-thing to remind me of my vanquisher; but

*the shoe that I hold has be worn by the di-
vinity that Lussanville will forever adore, it
is his most precious possession. He will not
return it before he has your word. Will you
excuse him, Mademoiselle?... No; if you hate
him, & if another... But if your heart speaks
for me, you will view this too free act merely
as a token of my most ardent love.*

— *LUSSANVILLE*

"Fanchette," said the merchant woman, after the beautiful Florangis had read this letter, "Do you forgive him?"

"Yes, Madame," responded the young person.

And no less than content, her good mistress entered the boutique.

M. Apatéon was sick with rage for not having recovered Fanchette: his housekeeper came that very same day to apprise her ward of this interesting bit of news. The kind Florangis spoke of Lussanville & showed her his letter.

"Another note," said the good Néné! "Eh, but!... How's that!... Verily... I have the best opinion in the world of this young Lussanville."

"Are you telling me the truth, my nanny?"

"Yes, but don't take my word for it, men..."

"Men, – what about them?"

"If you only knew how different they all are!"

"Are they like M. Apatéon?"

"Ah! really, that would not be half bad, if they

all resembled him; but while one acts like St. Nitouche,[16] another pretends to have feelings, to be sincere, to be the most faithful person in the world; you
can trust him; he wants nothing, but demands
everything. This other one will go hang himself if you
don't love him, he will throw himself in the river, or
at the very least he will die languishing; the same person, one week later, wants nothing more to do with
you, and looks on you with indifference. This kind of
man treats love cavalierly; but he espies the occasion,
like the cat watches the mouse. He is seen to express
great feelings, to fulminate against men who deceive
girls, & all that, my dear Fanchette, so as to better deceive them. There are those who launch their attack
brusquely, & who tell you the first time they meet
you that they love you, while displaying an audacity
that proves the exact opposite. Finally, one finds
sometimes a lover who puts himself in our shoes, &
acts precious; he adroitly exposes to our view
whatever is most valuable to him, & quite a bit more
even; he's a coquette in a doublet; would you believe
that these vile eccentrics have the skill to lure us into
their nets? Alas! my dear child, I would not believe it
had I not seen it with my own two eyes; but one
learns at one's own expense: all these men I've described have deceived me."

The governess had moist eyes on saying these
words, & she swore from the bottom of her heart that
they would not deceive the young Florangis. Then
they exited together, for some shopping that the good
Néné wanted to do for her dear girl. A long mantelet,
an immense hood, covered the young person, in such
a way that she was veiled like a Turkish woman, who

---

[16] St. Nitouche: a person who pretends wisdom or devotion, who
affects innocence and modesty.

goes outside the house to visit the public baths: but Fanchette attracted attention; all eyes were fixed on her pretty foot: she didn't pass by a single man whose heart was not moved by it; not one woman whose bile was not roused by it; not one person whose admiration was not excited by it.

When they were at the clothing merchant's shop, the workers, instead of listening to the old Néné, stared at Fanchette's foot, & if the orders of the master of the place hadn't torn them from their ecstasy, perhaps the good woman & her charge would not have obtained so quickly the cloth he sold to them. When they saw the kind Florangis' face, their admiration was not increased; they said: "My how beautiful she is! but it's wasted on her."

This was at the shop of an old man, a former neighbor of Fanchette's father, where the good woman had brought her. He was struck by the charms of this Fanchtette no less than the young men were. Néné told him that she was the daughter of his old colleague. The old man, surprised, looked at her closer, said that he remembered her, & wanted to embrace her: Fanchette side-stepped the accolade; but he took hold of her hand anyways; he pressed it rather roughly, while the governess picked up, turned over, put back, various rolls of fabric, & didn't find anything suitable for her ward.

"My dear neighbor, I remember seeing you as a child; I feel such a tender affection for you that you can put it to the test; everything you see here is yours, & I have no other desire than to treat you as a father & as a friend."

He reminded Fanchette of M. Apatéon; she made a deep curtsey, & thanked him kindly.

"You must accept my offer, my beautiful child; I will treat you like my daughter, & I will find a good husband for you."

With this, Fanchette found she was at fault; Apatéon had never spoken of marriage to her; she would have been quite charmed if someone had married her to Lussanville; with that lover, who was so gentle, so tender, who treated like a treasure whatever she had touched: but as she was prudent, she thanked the merchant again, & drew near to her nanny.

While they were shown more fabric, two young libertines, who had been following them since they left the fashion merchant's shop, entered & had cloth shown to them, as they stood next to Néné & Fanchette: in the merchant's shop, nothing but Fanchette was to their liking; also, they looked only at her, not at the cloth. If Fanchette stayed put, they admired her dazzling beauty; if she took a step, their eyes followed her & her pretty little foot: they tried several times to engage her in conversation: Fanchette responded with modesty, but she responded merely in monosyllables, & then broke away from them.

Finally, the good Néné settled on a roll of satin, which the old man had gone himself to fetch from a room apart. Never had they seen anything of such fine quality: across a pearl-white background ran a green & pink design, from which lilac & silver flowers stood out. The price he was asking for it was so modest that the beautiful Florangis & her nanny thought the merchant must surely have made a mistake; they said as much to him. But he put their minds at ease. The two young libertines & the shop hands all exclaimed in concert: "Oh! how charming that cloth will be, when she embellishes it!"

Chapter XVII

From which great things must follow.

Néné had never been so happy in her life: she paid for the cloth, & she carried the fabric; Fanchette was holding some other trifles in her arms: but either it was because of the old man winking to them, or on their own initiative, the shop assistants took the goods out of their hands, in spite of themselves, & offered to carry it home for them.

"My you're charming, Mademoiselle!" said the pleasanter of the two, who escorted Florangis. "I would consider myself happy, if you would permit me to pay you a visit sometime, & to introduce myself better to you. I am rich, from a good family; my ancestors are cloth merchants from over a century ago: I was placed with M. Delaunage because the merchandise he sells is mine: you can see just what a profitable & well-run establishment it is: my mother adores me: everything I want becomes a rule for her; besides, your name is well-known; Monsieur your father was ruined, but he didn't owe a single *sol*[17] to anyone; his honor remains completely in tact amongst the body of merchants: consent to become my companion, and I'll return you to a state that you were born into."

This young man spoke quite reasonably, & Fanchette loved his logic. Dolsans hadn't measured up to Lussanville for a single moment: Satinbourg (that's the name of this young merchant) intended to sweep her off her feet, not by inclination, but by affinity, sweet equality, & love of a prior state. The young girl responded kindly: "Monsieur, I'm grateful for the sentiments you show me; but I have a fear of

---

[17] *sol*: old form of *sous*. In English, a penny.

engagement, & strong reasons make it a law for me not to think about it just yet; you may not visit me; that would not be seemly: but speak with my nanny." These last words satisfied the young merchant.

The young man who was escorting the governess was busy as well.

"That young demoiselle depends on you, Madame," he said to her: "If you were at all interested in finding her an honest match, I'm at your service. An older brother of mine just passed away; my father, to whose business I will return, lives on rue Saint-Antoine. His boutique is worth at least as much as M. Delaunage's: he is old now, disabled, wants to retire, & will hand it all over to me: but don't take my word for it, go see for yourself, check it out; his name is Damasville: I prefer Mlle. Florangis to any girl from the richest of families, & I would do my utmost to make her happy." "You are very honorable, Monsieur," responded the good Néné. And they arrived.

While the governess relayed to her charge the propositions made by Damasville, the two young libertines, having arrived before them, were speaking to the fashion merchant. One was the Count d'A***, the other was the Marquis C***; both of them were charming, rich, masters in their own right. Their intentions were not honest like that of Lussanville, but they were powerful; in a matter of moments, they made an offer to the merchant woman to secure her niece's fortune, & to make her a girl of consequence: it was merely a matter, they said, of putting aside an honor of prejudice, in exchange for something infinitely more convenient & of greater value in society. The merchant woman (& also of fashion!), raised among the Ostrogoths, was not familiar with that honor; she assured them she would never consent to such an exchange, & she asked them seriously to drop it.

Chapter XVIII

A pack of suitors.

During M. Apatéon's illness, which was long, Fanchette & her nanny went outside sometimes. Néné thought it would be good to have her ward visit some of her parents' acquaintances, who were unknown to M. Apatéon, & whom she esteemed the most; with the design that Fanchette's uncle, on his return to France, would have less trouble finding the beautiful orphan, his niece. The earlier misfortunes of M. Florangis, her father, had made ingrates of all his friends; his daughter's pretty little foot turned them all into criminals. There was not an old man among them who didn't try to seduce her, not a young man who didn't undertake to touch her.

Lussanville hadn't missed a single occasion to see his mistress when she exited; but it was impossible, by the manner in which Fanchette covered her head, for her to notice him. One day, he could not resist the desire to say something to her: he timidly approaches the nanny, & greets his lover: on hearing his voice, Fanchette's heart trembles; she blushes while looking at him. The young Lussanville spoke of his feelings; he was so honest, so persuasive; he expressed himself in so touching a manner, that Néné herself found pleasure listening to him. He offered to accompany them; the nanny accepted: for the first time, that passionate lover touched Fanchette's beautiful arm; he offered to hold her hand: the girl was vividly touched, her knees trembled, & her heart said: "Dear Lover! Will you be faithful?" But she kept her mouth shut. What a happy state she was in! If she hadn't felt a little fear, it would have been less delicious.

Dolsans, no less amorous, visited Fanchette every day at his aunt's boutique: having the same name as her seemed to grant him certain rights of familiarity: however, he could never obtain the permission to accompany her. He had no doubt about Lussanville's passion: the merchant woman didn't hide from him the Marquis de C***'s propositions: the young painter shuddered; he resolved to follow his mistress as soon as she exited, to rush to her aid when need arose. Insofar as he never heard the praises of Fanchette except by strangers, his jealous nature had suffered much less than his love had been flattered; but when he recognized Lussanville, he could no longer contain himself. On seeing him approach Fanchette & her nanny, who received him with a familiar & satisfied air, a thousand dreadful designs passed through his mind. Insensate! he didn't know that one must not dispute with the heart of a beautiful woman, except by striving to surpass one's rival in virtues, in talents, in love! Dolsans proposed to attack Lussanville as soon as he quit the beautiful Florangis & Néné's side; but the young man entered with them into the house they were visiting, only adding to his pain & jealousy.

It was to a relative of Fanchette's mother that Néné brought her ward. This woman received them coldly at first; but when Lussanville confided in the good lady what he felt for her young cousin, & after he apprised her of his plans to marry her, she changed her tune, & she gave the girl a thousand caresses: a future companion of M. de Lussanville was quite another thing in her eyes, than the young & poor Fanchette. When they were about to leave, the nanny exhorted Lussanville not to accompany them; they returned home alone, unfortunately.

On arriving at the fashion merchant's house, they found a pack of suitors, who seemed to have spread the word around. Satinbourg & Damasville were the first to present themselves before Fanchette. They begged her to decide between them. The young Florangis had just come away from seeing Lussanville: she assured them both that she wanted to remain single for a long time still, & begged them to stop visiting her. The nanny & the merchant woman, for their part, had sent away a young lawyer who was beginning to make a name for himself at court, by ornate speeches for the defense, in the *ruelle* style; a young prosecutor, who felt his conscience burdened, because his father had overloaded Fanchette's father, who was his neighbor, with unjust expenses in order to drive him into bankruptcy & purchase for a song the unfortunate man's pretty house; Apatéon's nephew, who ardently desired the voluptuous Bigot's death, but who paid, even more than his uncle did, that fatal tribute to nature; a government functionary, who wanted a pretty companion for himself, to use her to woo his patrons, & to move up more rapidly in the world; & twenty other men, all children of those who had looked with an indifferent or satisfied eye on her father's ruin. The nanny Néné was walking on cloud nine.

"My dear child," she said, "pick & choose; but don't follow your heart except when it speaks in concert with reason."

"Nanny?... Lussanville?"

"Behold the man you prefer; he deserves it, dear Fanchette, if he's faithful; but will he be?"

"I believe so, nanny."

"One must believe nothing, & doubt everything."

"Not taking into account my perfect devotion, Madame," said the Marquis de C***, who had drawn near without their noticing it & insinuated himself into their conversation: "I possess rank, titles, powerful relatives; I am sincere, young, tender; I don't tell you that I will marry Mademoiselle, I will be a mentor instead; but outside of that, when she makes a wish, I will fulfill it, without hesitation, without argument; her fortune will cost her but a nod of the head, her tastes, her fantasies, her caprices will be laws to me; a brilliant equipage, diamonds, jewels, a delicious little house, one hundred other things that I do not mention, – all that is not something to be sneezed at... just one word, & she will have it all: there are a thousand men who cannot stand repeating themselves; but with you, it is different; one will wait on your resolutions; will one week suffice? Speak? I could go as long as two weeks: don't do something you'll regret, by refusing a honest man of leisure, who comes wooing you... I don't ask you to respond today; I will come again. Adieu, my adorable woman, until we meet again." He bowed with a flourish & proceeded to leave.

All that was spoken with so much volubility, that it was impossible to get a word in edgewise.

"Eh! Don't bother, Monsieur, coming back again," cried the governess after him, on seeing him disappear; "I tell emphatically today even, – a king's crown, in exchange for what you demand, will never tempt us." The marquis pretended not to hear her, & went away.

An equipage stopped at the door at this moment: out came a short, fat man. Fanchette let out a cry of fright; she thought it was M. Apatéon. He draws near; casts a protective look over everything, & sits down wheezing.

"Is this your beautiful child?" he said to the merchant woman. "She is rather... fine," he added, looking the young Florangis up and down with a cheeky look on his face. "Tell me, my girl, haven't I seen you somewhere before?" Fanchette lowered her gaze & blushed. "In all honesty, I find she has got an innocent attitude. I will get used to it. Ah, Heaven!... eh! My beautiful puppet! What a pretty gem you have there. No, come to think of it, I'm mistaken, you are not the same person I had seen at the Saint-Cloud Ballroom: I would have noticed that pretty little foot there. It's more true than ever, than 3 times 3 makes six, plus 4 makes ten, that you are a perfection... But, where is she going? Listen, listen to me, young woman! I mean no harm to you... Call her back, then; she's not listening to me!"

The governess had never had a Financier as a lover; she barely understood what he was talking about. The merchant woman, more knowledgeable, answered him in a cold tone of voice: "Monsieur, you are mistaken; it's not my place that someone will have directed you to. Look elsewhere."

"Indeed, by golly! I do find you amusing: my officer & agent led me astray! Me! That young person is not named Fanchette? She isn't your apprentice?

She's not pretty, an orphan, & poor? & by consequence, the girl I'm after?"

"Eh, why, Monsieur, why are you 'after her'
as you put it?" said the governess flat out.

"Good question! Because she's pretty; because I like pretty women, & because I pay them
handsomely..."

"Leave, Monsieur," retorted at the same time
both the merchant woman & Néné. "Leave, I tell you.
I cannot summon any more of my indignation: look
elsewhere for the unfortunate victims of your debauchery..."

"Adieu, my beautiful ladies, adieu: the young
woman will maybe be more malleable: adieu. You are
enraged; but you see quite clearly that one will no
longer address himself to you: your time is over.
Adieu." He departs, with these last words, & leaves
the good Néné very scandalized by his brutal blunt-
ness.

Chapter XIX

Wherein Fanchette is modest & generous.

Pudor had obliged Fanchette to escape: she locked
herself in her room with the young Agathe. The good
girl reflected on that pack of suitors who asked for her
hand: as for the others, like the impudent Financier,
the Count, the Marquis, &c., she didn't give them a
second thought. She returned to her work, & labored.
"We deserve to be the wife of Lussanville," she told
herself: "I have no possessions; I cannot become his
equal but by my virtue. My father traced this out for

me, the route that I must follow, very clearly: it's only by executing faithfully his last commands that I will be worthy of my lover." A tender sigh followed this modest reflection of hers.

Fanchette was calm: a piercing cry, let out by the merchant woman, drew her out of her sweet revery: the two girls shudder, & fly to her. What a spectacle before their eyes! Dolsans, carried in by four men; his blood leaving his body through a large wound: Lussanville, shedding tears, is not far behind!

"You see a guilty party, Mademoiselle," said the young painter to Fanchette, as soon as he caught sight of her, "whom Heaven punishes: I loved you, I adore you even to my dying breath, but I'm not worthy of you, because I've become a criminal... I have just attacked a man whom you prefer to me. I would have taken his life remorselessly maybe, & I see him shedding tears for the fate I deserve...."

He becomes silent; & the sobs stifled the kind & tender Florangis.

"Ah! Madame! " she said to the merchant woman finally, "I'm the one to blame for this misfortune! Dolsans! If I could redeem your days at the expense of my happiness & my life... Yes, Madame," she added, looking at her mistress; "would that he might live... do all you can to save him; & if he must have my hand in marriage, if that's what it takes to make him want to live, I will not listen to my heart, which speaks to me in support of his rival; I promise my hand, & I will give it to him."

Lussanville heard this cruel decree: "Ah, Fanchette!" he said to her in a half-voice, "you loved me! & I lose you! If had known there was no place for me between death & this reversal, I would not have defended my life, which was furiously attacked. My destiny then is decided. A hand tainted by blood will not join itself to yours... Adieu. I will die."

"Don't make me more miserable than I already am. I loved you, I love you; but I will no longer be able to say it to you, to see you. If you were in Dolsans place, I would no longer be alive."

"O Heaven! Who would have thought, that I would be miserable upon hearing that flattering avowal!" Overwhelmed with sorrow, desperate, the young lover went away weeping.

Dolsans' wound was not so dangerous as they had at first imagined: his aunt, reassured, caressed Fanchette, repeating to her, that far from accusing her of the evil done to her nephew, she was about to owe her her happiness & her life. The young Agathe joined in with her mother; she hugged the kind Florangis: "How happy I will be to call you my cousin for reals!" she said to her. Fanchette wept: but she didn't repent her self-sacrifice; her generous soul performed a good act, without suffering her to savor the sweetness of it.

Chapter XX

The foot slips: she falls.

Kathégètes, that respectable old man, Lussanville's governor, was struck by the sad demeanor of his charge. But he made it a maxim never to ask questions: he assumed only a sweet & kind demeanor, more marked than ordinary, so as to encourage his charge's confidence in him. He was all the more surprised by Lussanville's reserve, & to see him determined to accomplish a plan formed long ago to tour the principal countries of Europe: the young man seemed previously to envisage this trip with repugnance, & had completely discarded the thought of it from the moment he met the beautiful Florangis. M. Kathégètes felt sure that something extraordinary had happened; he noticed that everything bored Lussanville; that he felt ill at ease everywhere he went. "He's in love," said the good man; "but he wants to escape! I would like to know what a young man, so well suited for love, found cruel." Curiosity got the better of him & his principles.

"What is it that's eating you?" he said one day to the kind young man.

"Ah! Father!... I love, I was loved... & yet, I'm miserable!"

"You answer a question that's been bothering me by engendering it with another."

"Stop asking; it will only make matters worse." And the old man fell silent. His ward was tormented; he squandered his time among assemblies of people; then suddenly he made an about face, shutting himself off from the world in absolute solitude; but the dart was lodged in his heart; his pain followed him everywhere. He often visited the good Néné, who tried to console him, telling him to stop despairing. He begged her to accept, on Fanchette's behalf, the present he had made: at first she refused; then she gave in, & the tender young man felt less unhappy.

Fanchette's other lovers were not discouraged: M. Delaunage every day sent new gifts that were refused; Satinbourg & Damasville could not obey the order to stop visiting her: the Marquis & the Count continued to make dazzling promises; but the Financier took another route. One day the good Florangis exited a church: a carriage was barring the portal. Fanchette makes an attempt to walk around it: two big lackeys grab her by the arms, put her inside against her will, shut the doors, & the carriage hurries off. When they stopped, the young person found herself within the courtyard of a magnificent mansion: she's led into a sumptuous furnished apartment: she had barely arrived when who enters the room, but the massive & plump individual who spoke to her so cavalierly at her mistress' boutique.

"My queen," he said to her, approaching, "do not be afraid; you are free here; it's not my custom to use violence against beautiful women."

"To prove to me that what you say is true, Monsieur, permit me to leave at once."

"My goodness! Not so fast! at least hear me out first. Why play the prude & be so unsociable? In truth, my child, if you keep that mania up, you will never see the light of day; &, pretty as you are, that would be a real shame: you could have anything you wanted. Do you want, by a legitimate & ceremonious marriage, to bury yourself with a lout? My faith! that's not my advice. I want to enlighten you, counsel you; I speak to you as a friend. Come on, little one... But why! You have to realize you'll be making a terrible mistake... calm down a bit. Sit down here."

"No, Monsieur: I want to leave."

"No, beautiful puppet, just a moment... Eh! Let me see that little foot of yours: it's so pretty! Why hide it?"

"I don't deserve this, Monsieur, no, I don't deserve it, this humiliation."

"Huh? Who do you say is humiliating you! Listen to me, girl: this charm here can alone make you your fortune, & I will confess to you that, for me, it is what most pleases me about you. My dear child, do not think that I want you to grow old with me: I change often; I possess treasures; I share them with those I quit: everyone knows I have good taste: to have had me is like a title for finding a new lover."

"I don't want your riches, nor a lover."

"I know more about your affairs than you think, beautiful Fanchette; you are going to marry an oaf you don't love, & you push away a lover you do: I know everything; here's what I propose. In one week you will marry Lussanville, my sister's son, & my pupil; I will provide you with a rich dowry: is there nothing in this that tempts you?"

"Alas! Monsieur, I have promised to marry Dolsans, to sacrifice myself, to save his life, & I will keep my promise."

"Ah! This time, my belle, I no longer understand. What! You didn't love Lussanville then?"

"Forgive me..."

"And you refuse him?"

"Yes, Monsieur."

"The reason, if you please, for this rare manner of proceeding?"

"It's because sooner or later, I will occasion Dolsans' death, or his, & I'm not keen on either, paying too dearly for a single person's life at the expense even of my honor."

"But tell me, honestly, what cave have you been living in? My faith, dear girl, the Romans have touched you in the head. You must cure yourself of that. To the effect that, under seal of the most inviolable secret, you would be adamantly opposed to granting me anything, not a single taste, not a nibble, in order to receive the hand of my nephew, & the assurance of succeeding to all my riches."

"Ah, Heaven! What a horror!"

"She's frightened! Ah! I will heal her of that." he said laughing.

To proceed with his cure, marvelous according to him, the Financier overwhelmed Fanchette with his heavy mass, & began dutifully to ravish her favors, the least of which had a price well & above the value of all his treasures. The good girl, like so many others before her, could have ceded to the violence; but she was honest-to-god virtuous; she escaped; the heavy *Midas* pursued her: just as formerly Syrinx fled before Pan, the inventor of the panpipe.[18] Fanchette, out of breath, called for help at the top of her lungs; but what help could she hope for in a house purchased for crime? Overcome with lassitude, shaking, her foot slips, she falls; the Financier advances a canopy, which catches her. Before she can get up, he's at her feet again; he takes hold of them; he kisses them a million times: All Fanchette's efforts to escape him now are useless. She breaks down in tears.

"O! My father!" she exclaimed, "your daughter has hit a snag; she is about to lose her innocence;

---

[18] Syrinx... panpipe: Syrinx was a nymph, in Greek mythology, who was renowned for her chastity, and was pursued by the god Pan. In flight, she ran to a river, and was metamorphosied into reeds, which the god, desolate, cut and made into a panpipe (known as a syrinx).

but she's not here for her imprudence. What then! A wicked man can soil the purest soul, just like that!" She had barely finished speaking when someone banged loudly at the door: the Financier got up; he hesitates, but finally, seeing that whoever it was banged again more loudly, he opens the door himself: it's Lussanville: Fanchette runs into his arms.

"Save the woman you have loved," she cries; "Free her from the hands of a brute, whom my tears cannot dissuade..." At this moment of pain & indignation, Lussanville plants his mouth onto Fanchette's, who does not turn her face away; he carries her away, far from that loathsome person's residence.

Chapter XXI

Fanchette loses one of her slippers.

Lighter on his feet than Zephyr, when by his breath he gently stirs the stems of flowers, Lussanville with precious load, gained his carriage: Fanchette's frightened air was observed by two passersby, who at that moment found themselves in front of the Financier's residence. One of them in particular, deeply struck by the young person's traits, looked at her with interest. His eyes are fixed on that little foot of hers, that a cute slipper half-contained. The emotion that stirred in him by this seductive foot & that delicate slipper made his heart tremble. Equally touched by the young & beautiful girl, whom they believed violence was being done to, the two of them rush forward to assist her. The beautiful Florangis, who mistook them for the Financier's henchmen, leaps precipitously into Lussanville's carriage: the two unknown men, who imagined she was being forced against her will, seize her by the dress:

"Dear friend!" screamed Fanchette, & her arms wrap around Lussanville. At such a sweet name given to the charming young man, her two liberators freeze, look at each other, & conclude that with such a face as his, one is never reduced to forcing girls to do something they didn't wish to. But Fanchette's pretty slipper had tempted the more forward of the two strangers: in the precipitous agitations that the good girl had made to escape his grip, her shoe came free; the stranger was able to pay himself back for his trouble by slipping off the gem that charmed him; he takes possession of it adroitly, slips it into his pocket, pays a flattering compliment to the young beauty, explains what they were thinking when they approached; they were answered by a deep bow, & the carriage departs in a flash.

The two strangers appeared to be foreigners: in fact, one was a rich inhabitant of the French colonies in Asia; the other, the governor of his only son, whom this particular person had sent back to France several years earlier. The son had disappeared one day, just like that, at a moment in time when he was seized by a violent passion for a woman: his governor wore himself out in vain trying to find him: disheartened, despairing, he took it upon himself to bring word of his ward back to the father; news of so great a misfortune did not sit well with him. The two men had only just returned to France several days before.

"What a treasure!" said the Asiatic Frenchman to his son's instructor. In the state I find myself, only a girl as beautiful as she is could mollify the bitterness cast on the rest of my life: yes, I would bless

Heaven to have met her, if I didn't think he was her husband. But who knows? Maybe she was only his mistress? Unfortunately, all the means of making certain of this are lacking."

"Be that as it may," said the governor, "you should abandon pursuit, that young person being either married or unworthy to look on you."

"Unworthy to look on me! Now see here, my old friend, look at this slipper, & represent for yourself the traits of the girl who wore it. Look, I said!"

"At forty years old, you! Seduced by a pretty little foot! Ah! ah..."

"'Ah!' yourself. You who laugh so heartily, could you resist her? No, I didn't think so. It's decided; I must discover her name, her fortune: we have done our utmost to find an unfortunate family that I left behind... in misery: all that was left was a girl; you heard it yourself that nobody knows what's become of her. And just now we have seen with our own two eyes an example of what doubtless caused the unfortunate necessity that brought me back to France again, where I will likely die looking for him. My son, believing himself master of himself, will have scorned your authority, given himself over to dissoluteness, & will have gone off & disappeared. My relatives will have lost all hope in me... We are going to make a renewed effort: if all is in vain, at least this young beauty should be freed, whatever she may have done prior to now; I will not hesitate. How many are there, of this bewitching sex, who, seduced by a perfidious fellow, led by example, often set free by what should be keeping them & protecting them, remain virtuous at the very bosom of libertinage! For, as you know, clearly, virtue does not consist in holding onto a flower that an honest woman was forced to give away: it all depends on how it is lost: eh! What can we reproach them with? No, I don't call it a crime, a condition they could not avoid, no; & I would not esteem any less this young person who has just charmed me off my feet: my hand, my fortune, I will offer it all to her, I will give it all way: her empire over my heart is absolute; there it is, my friend, there it is; & if unfortunately I should find out she is married... I've never felt this before, what I feel for her now, I can't say I would respond with my virtue."

And as they discoursed in this manner, the two friends continued walking down the road in the direction that Lussanville's carriage had taken. They stop by chance before the house he occupied, & recognize one of the domestics who was just a moment earlier accompanying Fanchette's young lover. They approach him to interrogate him: but Lussanville was loved by his people; they didn't say anything about their master that wasn't good, & never spoke ill of his actions: this domestic turned away from them, without saying a word.

The stranger learned nothing at this time; but one of them couldn't hide the joy he felt on having found the residence of the happy lover, with whom, there was no doubt in his mind, the girl with the pretty little foot lived. He withdrew, with the resolution to stop at nothing in the discovery of the fate of the beautiful girl whose pretty slipper he had stolen (& there was nothing more sensual & exciting than that slipper; it was sky blue, embellished with a silver netting); he could never grow tired of looking at this gem, the sight of which touched him to the quick & revived his sensual desires for the fairer sex.

Part Two

Chapter XXII

Presents that will become famous.

Meanwhile in the carriage, Lussanville, transported with joy for having rescued his lover from the cynical audacity of an opulent libertine, held her in his arms, & said to her: "Dear Fanchette, without the unhappiness that banished me faraway from you, you would have been lost. Ready to leave Paris, I wanted to see you one more time this morning: I noticed that you had gone outside alone: if your nanny, or your young companion had been with you, I would not have hesitated to approach you; but you were alone; I was afraid to displease you. In church, I was behind you. Fortunately, I recognized my uncle's loathsome henchman, when you were abducted. I flew after you: it was necessary to wreck violence on the flunkies who serve him & who imitate him in his vices, before reaching those secret apartments consecrated to seduction & debauchery. I bless my misfortune, which saves the thing I love. But, alas!... must I leave you?"

"My heart breaks; yes, leave: leave, dear lover, as you have resolved; I demand it; but do not despair anymore."

"Heaven! What am I hearing? Beautiful Fanchette! You give me life again..." His mouth was glued to his lover's hand: then he raised his eyes: they both stopped speaking, but gazed at each other, so tenderly! Lussanville dried the tears that continued to flow. They arrived at his house. Fanchette was afraid to enter the house of her lover; but her slipper was lost, & her appearance was in a strange disorder; she was anxious not to return home & appear in crumpled & creased clothing before Dolsans' jealous & penetrating eyes; she said to Lussanville:

"I trust your good intentions," & she gave him her hand. He helped her out of the carriage. The beautiful Florangis had no reason to repent of it. The kind Lussanville was floating on a cloud of joy to see the queen of his soul at his house.

"Why must you leave," he said, "from this place where you will reign one day! Divinity of my heart! It is here where I will cherish you, adored by the most gentle of husbands."

Fanchette smiled: joy began to reanimate her battered soul. She had her portrait, which Dolsans had recently made of her during his convalescence, & which Lussanville was flattered to receive from Fanchette's hand; it was in the same box as that of her mother's portrait; she added a bracelet, which she had braided herself from her own hair; & these presents were for Lussanville. She asked him for her pretty shoe back; but that was only to put it in the box for him. Lussanville, for his own part, asked her to accept a pair of magnificently embroidered slippers, made according to the design he held in his hands; Fanchette had need of his present; but it pleased her independently of that; she didn't hide her feelings at all: she accepted also the box of jewels that her lover had asked the good Néné to keep; she promised him that she would adorn herself with his gifts. Innocent & precious favors! Ah, what charms you hold for tender hearts! The kind young man, filled with gratitude, said to his charming mistress: "My adorable spouse, surely we will owe the greatest part of our possessions to our misfortunes."

After having examined Fanchette's portrait, Lussanville cast a glance at Madame Florangis' portrait; he was surprised to find her so richly clad: He was going to kiss it; he let out a cry: "I can't believe it!" he said to his lover, "here is the image of the woman who brought you into the world! O Heaven! But you become more dear to me now. Yes, divine Fanchette, & like father like son... the same power subjected them. But my father's passion was illegitimate, & was as unfortunate as it was extreme. If he had been a witness to the ruin of her whom he adored, he would have repaired the wrong; instead, his son is bound to do it. Beautiful Florangis! What new bonds would this discovery not make, if something could augment my attachment to you!" Lussanville kissed the portrait: "Kind mother of my bride," he said, "yes, I adore you too! You are accused of having taken my father from me; but you give me a companion who will make my happiness." Fanchette listened to Lussanville with astonishment; but she didn't interrogate him. They looked at each other, & grew emotional over their parents' fate; they spoke about how much they had loved them, & they knew that their parents' good & sensitive hearts resembled their own.

Finally, the kind Florangis, having been rescued from the cruel assault she had just escaped, accompanied (at a distance) by her lover, returned to her mistress' home: her presence calmed the fashion merchant's heightened anxieties, & put an end to the young Agathe's alarms.

Chapter XXIII

Not all truths are good to speak out loud.

Dolsans had recovered; & Lussanville, in obedience to Fanchette's wishes, stayed faraway. Fanchette, on seeing her nanny again, apprised her of her new arrangements. The governess loved Lussanville; she was devastated to learn about her ward's generous resolution, but didn't argue with her: she made it known at that time how happy she was; then the horrible danger that Fanchette had just run into made her shudder. Meanwhile, M. Apatéon was beginning to get out & about. The young Florangis needed to be very careful when she went outside.

The painter was looking forward to unadulterated bliss. If Fanchette received him coldly, he placed his hopes on everything one could expect from a beautiful soul when she was reminded of her duty. He pressed for their union: the merchant woman backed her nephew up, & the young Florangis felt it was all over for her: she didn't know that with M. Apatéon being her tutor, named in her father's will, & the governess substituted for him by a secret codicil, they could do nothing without their consent: she saw no other way to escape irreparable unhappiness, than the imprudent admission of her engagement to Lussanville: she did it without consulting her nanny. Dolsans was furious. Fanchette learned then what violence a jealous person is capable of; she was afflicted, tormented, until the moment when Néné, having learned about everything, was able to speak with the merchant woman firmly, threatening to take Fanchette away from her, if she could not protect her from Dolsans' persecutions. "How's that! Mother," said the young Agathe, "my cousin would be the cause of my losing my friend! If I thought that were true, I would no longer love him."

If the faults committed by a jilted lover weren't excusable, Dolsans would be a monster. He persuaded himself that if he ended up ravishing Fanchette, taking the flower of her innocence, he could obtain her hand easily; he adored her; he downplayed in his mind the atrocity of this premeditated act, by the motive for committing it. From the moment he had settled on this culpable plan, he seemed calm: he saw Fanchette, but didn't speak with her about his love; he hid it in his heart, & as he repressed his desires, they only acquired more violence.

One Sunday, Dolsans didn't come round: Fanchette, delighted by his absence, put on for the first time the dress bought at M. Delaunage's; she did herself up more than usual, seized the occasion to fulfill her promise to Lussanville to emphasize her beauty by the diamonds she had received from him; she slipped on that pretty slipper that he himself had designed, & committed a new imprudence. She was walking on cloud nine: every step she took called her dear Lussanville to mind. For the first time in her life, she admired the elegance of her pretty foot. "Ah! If Lussanville was only here," she said to herself, "how flattered I would be! Dear lover! If I hadn't been seen by anyone, I would not have been yours! I don't want to please anyone but you, for my heart loves you & desires only you!" Then she walked; & her heart fluttered. "I'm all Lussanville's," she told herself; "it's he, the dear object of my feelings, who embellishes me." These agreeable ideas filled Fanchette's face with a cheerful expression, & made her beauty even more resplendent, when Dolsans showed up.

He sees the gifts of his rival; he grows pale; he dissimulates his rage (it was still a fault of his that he had brought back with him from Italy, that of dissimulation: alas! We pick up our neighbor's vices, & we leave their virtues; the sad memento that an infinite number of young men keep from their travels) & he swears that Fanchette will not get away from him. However, at the bottom of his heart, born virtuous, as her extremely touching beauty excited his remorse, he pulls himself aside: "What are you doing, miserable Dolsans?" he asked himself, "& why do you want to force yourself on a lovely creature who does not willingly give her love to you? She is beautiful, tender; I adore her: must all that be used against her? Be reasonable: let her go: if she loves you, she'll come back again; we merit her esteem & her friendship. It's all over: I'm leaving. Another man, before my very eyes, will take possession of a good more dear to me than my life! She promised me! She no longer wants to... She was sacrificing herself; I was not loved. So be it." Virtue got the upper hand in his mind; until his eyes fell on that seductive foot of hers, newly embellished by a masterpiece of footwear design; he went out of his mind when he saw it. "Huh! I would give that up?!" his mind raced: "No; *iacta alea est.*[19] I may end up culpable, but I will be less miserable, maybe."

The fashion merchant & her girls were supposed to go out & take some air in the countryside: carriages awaited them out front; they were about to depart, when the governess arrived. Her admiration, on sight of the dear girl, burst out in a thousand ways: imprudent praises succeeded in pouring poison into Dolsans' soul. They leave: Agathe has already departed: Fanchette, who sees that the young painter must

---

[19] *iacta alea est*: Latin for "the die is cast."

accompany them in the same carriage, begs her nanny to help her get out of going; & Néné makes up some excuse for why they can't go. They return together to the house, just the two of them. Dolsans, whose jealousy gave him the eyes of a lynx, cast at the young Florangis, who was getting away, a furious look, followed up by a bitter smile.

Chapter XXIV

Peril that will make hearts shudder.

As soon as Fanchette was alone with her nanny, Lussanville became the subject of their conversation: the good girl spoke with modesty about the young man: her governess smiled; & when Fanchette least expected it, Néné handed her a letter that she had just received from that cherished lover.

LETTER FROM LUSSANVILLE TO FANCHETTE

– Bayonne, 30 March 1768.

As you wished, my adorable bride (yes, I believe I am allowed to call you this, from the moment you yourself rushed into my arms), I have quit the places you embellish by your presence; but I have read it in your heart: I am loved; I enjoy such inexpressible happiness, to be loved by the divine Fanchette: what an enchanting destiny! She suffers as much as I do, by an absence she orders. I don't grumble about the necessity of your action, my beautiful lover; I know the motive; it makes you dear to my heart!... Ah, my Fanchette! My charming bride! Call me back to you, my assistance will still be necessary to you perhaps. I don't know; but I shudder sometimes, for no reason at all: I imagine you in tears: I see you trembling, lost, desperate, raising your beautiful hands to heaven... Fanchette! This very night even, I thought I saw a traitor, with dagger in hand, asking for your heart. You were crying; I wanted to go to you. An invincible obstacle held me back. I let out a furious cry, & I woke up. True, it is only a dream, but a lover, who breathes for you alone, is frightened by the least of things: in the name of our love, in the name of the sacred bond that ought to unite us, dear bride, permit your groom to be close to you, to enjoy your presence: he cannot answer for your life, if he cannot obtain that grace. Adieu.

— *LUSSANVILLE*

When she was done reading it, Fanchette raised her moistened eyes to look at Néné: "He has departed then, nanny? He is faraway from me! It must be so, & at least, I have no more fear of bad things happening to him. What will we say to him, nanny?"

"Whatever your heart dictates."

"Ah! my heart desires nothing but him."

"Write to him. Tell him to return."

"Eh! But!... Dolsans, what if... however I would like to see him again."

"You decide: I'll respond to what he has written to me personally: you add a few words in your hand."

Letter from Fanchette,

at the bottom of the Governess' Letter,

to Lussanville

I take up the quill trembling: my nanny guides my hand... if you swear to me always to avoid Dolsans, then return. I'm so frightened! Alas! maybe the decision I make will be fatal to my lover! But he pressures me... come back, dear Lussanville! As I write to you, your bride is embellished by your gifts: I have refused to leave my room, for fear of being seen by your rival: all my companions, my dear Agathe above all, my nanny, my mistress, find me beautiful: I tell myself I owe this brilliance to Lussanville: why should my dear lover be deprived of seeing his work? What pleasure I take in keeping myself locked up, in hiding myself from other men's eyes! I want to be seen beautiful only in my groom's eyes... Return; but before you do, write to my nanny, & promise us both that you will keep yourself forever out of Dolsans' sight. He's a madman; I fear him as much as I love you. I'm all yours,

– Fanchette Florangis

It was that time of day when M. Apatéon was about to be returning home. They sealed this letter:

the governess brought it with her to post it, & she left her dear child alone, promising that she would return again as soon as the old man no longer had need of her services. Fanchette could not stop reading Lussanville's letter over again: she was holding it in her hand still when someone knocks; she runs to the door, thinking it was her nanny, but it is Dolsans. The good girl's face went pale, & she wanted to conceal her lover's letter.

"You returned alone, Monsieur?" she says, completely disturbed, to the young painter.

"Yes, cruel one," responds her furious lover, who had overheard the conversation she had earlier with her nanny. "I wanted to frustrate your desire to flee from me." And in so saying, he had the audacity to snatch the letter out of her hands. Indignant by such temerity, she demands it back, with a firm tone of voice; but in vain; he has already read it; he tears it up in a fit of rage.

At the mercy of a lover enraged by jealousy, the lovable girl shuddered.

"Are we alone?" asked Dolsans quietly. "You must choose to marry me, or... I will do something criminal, whatever you decide, you forced my hand; but what difference does it make? To follow you to the grave would be sweeter to me than seeing you in some rival's embrace."

"Fine!" said Fanchette, crying, "take my life then."

"O Heavens!" he thought to himself, "she'd rather die than be with me! Miserable wretch that I am!" Then, falling down on his knees, he blurts out: "Beautiful Fanchette, will I never be able to reach you, to touch your heart? You're driving me crazy!... Ah! But when we are man & wife, you will see then that these transports of mine, that are so hateful to you now, are a sign of the excess love I have for you. But, no, cruel girl, you prefer your lover to your life... Do not for one minute believe that he will escape my wrath: even if I have to pursue him to the ends of the earth, my blood-stained hands will exact vengeance on him for your unhappiness & my infamy."

"My God! Dolsans, stop!" she said, while in her mind she thought, "Eh! Here is the evil that my lover had a premonition of!" Then she said to him, "How can you think such horrors!"

"You, of all people, ask me about that, Fanchette! – love, love alone, which you outrage, makes me guilty of..."

"Love?! tender love! Oh! How can that be, if all you have is hate?"

"I would be generous enough to stifle it."

"You want my unhappiness or my death."

"Your unhappiness!? No, beautiful Fanchette. When we are married, you will see how I can love! Queen of my heart, deign only to wield your authority, & I swear to you I will make you happy."

"I will die of grief, if I lose Lussanville."

"Enough, cruel girl; & this tells me the path I must follow: sword, poison, rope, it does not matter: he will not escape."

"My soul leaves me: you are inhuman! Leave me, you make me sick! May Heaven help my lover, & I will ask him to punish you."

"That will not happen – at least, not until I've had my way..."

"Listen, Dolsans, don't; doesn't reason have any..."

"O, this is rich. You talk to me about reason! you who will do & say anything now, at this hour of present danger; you who break your promises, who filled me with the sweetest hopes, once upon a time."

Fanchette, who was young, & lacking in experience, thought her lover would be lost if at this very moment she didn't renounce again the hope of being with him: she felt she had to give in.

"Okay," she said to Dolsans, "because I have no choice; but it depends on M. Apatéon & my nanny: I cannot just give myself to you without their approval."

"Deceived again," retorted Dolsans, "How do you expect me to believe that? I need a security, something, that assures me of their consent."

"What would you have?" said Fanchette, with a tone of ingenuousness.

"Some proof that you will not go back on your word."

"Say it."

"You consent?"

"I have no choice." (She had no idea what he was going to ask for.) Dolsans wanted to take her into his arms; the girl pushes him away. He resorts to violence.

"O perfidy!" cried out Fanchette, struggling, "I abhor you; I would have any other miserable man in the world than you for my husband."

Dolsans (we have to confess) had no intention of making himself guilty of the horrible infamy he was menacing the beautiful & timid girl with; he only wished to frighten her, to oblige her to submit. He held her wrists with one hand, & with the other, he pulled out a knife: he positioned it at her bosom, while Fanchette shut her tear-filled eyes & said, "Just kill me then. O! Lussanville! If only you were here!"

These last words really irritated Dolsans: he looks at Fanchette in the face: he screams at her: "And this embellishment here, a gift by my rival, will increase the value of my conquest! Unfaithful girl! You have no fear of appearing too beautiful: you enhance your charms, & you want me to renounce my hopes of being the happy possessor of them! No, I swear to you – nothing can stop me now." And transported by his love, or by his anger, or by his lust, he was about to have his way with her when, Fanchette, frozen with fear, stops struggling, & despairs.

Chapter XXV

Fatal event.

That was it, clearly; & the occasion, his rage, his mistress' lack of resistance, they had all brought Dolsans to the verge of consummating his awful crime, if her governess had not returned in the nick of time. She calls out for her dear girl.

"Ah! My nanny!" cried out Fanchette, "to my rescue!"

Beside herself, Néné fills the house with her

cries. Two young men who were looking for any opportunity to see the beautiful Florangis again rush forward at the same moment: one was the Count d'A***; the other, the amorous Satinbourg. The door was no match for their efforts; they stove it in; but Dolsans, sword in hand, becomes a second barricade, more difficult to force: a crowd forms around the house: the Count d'A*** advances, Dolsans falls back; he wants to die; but he cannot support the thought that Fanchette will live for another man. The good girl, dying, frantic, reaches her hands out to her nanny who, braving the maniac's menaces, rushes forward, reaches her ward, & holds her tightly to her breast. The old Néné's courage saved Fanchette: Dolsans, by a crime (involuntary, no doubt) would have executed her probably; for having struck the governess, he lays himself wide open to the Count d'A***, who deals him a mortal blow.

Fanchette, covered in Néné's blood, had fainted; Satinbourg, frightened, attended to the both of them; the Count d'A*** explained the reason for his behavior to the Commandant of the Guard on horseback; & the fabric merchant, followed by Agathe, arrived home. When Fanchette refused to accompany them, she had noticed a change in the look on her nephew's face. While strolling along the way, she lost sight of him for several moments: the young girls, alive & playful, acting silly, after having been cooped up indoors for so long, diverted themselves, bounded o'er the grassy hillocks like tender lambs let out to graze in the fields on a beautiful spring day. This spectacle, one of naïve joy, the most charming of all, agreeably occupied the merchant woman's attention: only Agathe, who was missing her friend, seemed forlorn, & stood apart: she noticed Dolsans returning to Paris. She alerted her mother. The merchant woman was surprised when she learned of his departure; she felt feelings of fear; her heart tightened: she wanted to follow. How to describe her despair when, on entering her home again! she sees her nephew, & the pallor of death on his face. She lets out a piercing scream: she turns her head, & her eyes fall on Fanchette.

"Both of them!" she cried out, & her strength abandons her; she fell; the Count d'A*** caught her. And the young Agathe, more dead than alive, rushes to her friend's side.

Meanwhile, Asclepius' disciples came running to the scene as a result of the young Satinbourg's efforts. Their assistance was of no use for Dolsans; this miserable young man had just terminated a career that his last day had soiled. The nanny was superficially wounded in the arm; Fanchette reopens her beautiful eyes, & responds to the young Agathe's touching caresses; the merchant woman regains consciousness. Everyone looks at each other sighing.

"O! My child!" said the governess, "the things one must put up with to keep one's virtue!"

"My nanny," Fanchette replied, "what a fatal day!"

"You live, dear Fanchette?" called out the merchant woman; "ah, my dear child! You were entrusted to my care! he whom I loved, he was like a son to me... I'm told that by the most hateful crime he... He deserves his disastrous fate; but what about me, did I deserve the unhappiness that I now feel, which overwhelms me? Ah, cruel Dolsans! You were already lost to me, before you felt the fatal blow!"

The Count d'A*** & Satinbourg were both equally delighted to see Fanchette & her nanny free from danger: the fabric merchant felt, from the bottom of his heart, the joy of having been of service to the object of his feelings: they take Dolsans' body away, Satinbourg & the nanny herself, reassuring the lovable Florangis. How touching she looked in that disorderly state of mind, that the painter's attempt on her virtue had caused, & how interesting her suffering made her look! The Count d'A*** swore to do everything in his power to take possession of such a beautiful & good girl; Satinbourg promised himself to love her eternally. "Happy!" each of them said quietly to himself, "is he who will dry her tears! He who will make laughter & love appear again on that seductive little face!" Her governess could not be persuaded to leave Fanchette's side: however the hour was drawing near when she needed go back.

"Go, nanny," said the kind girl to her; "but before you do, to console me, tell me a thousand times that I will see him soon." Néné alone understood what she meant by this. And after she had consoled her, they separated. The Count d'A*** left, & Satinbourg escorted the governess home.

Chapter XXVI

Reflections.

"Alas, how a girl is beside herself smiling at her charms, in the mirror, when an elegant piece of clothing redoubles her splendor! She excites against her innocence a pack of enemies: finesse, gentleness, violence, love, they all come out to do her in. Feeble &

without experience, she succumbs, & becomes the object of contempt for those who have seduced her. O, my father! how wise you were, when you dressed your daughter in coarse fabric! You hid her, under that disagreeable, coarse tree bark, from the impudent eyes of seducers. They often disdain a victim who has nothing shimmering on: if one is not admired, feted, pursued, it means she has nothing that arouses their appetite. A thousand times happy is the girl whose prudent & cherished mother never leaves her alone! She spends her fortunate & tranquil days in the bosom of innocence: her mother looks out for her; she helps her steer clear of danger; she keeps her from deceptive discourses; she defends her against temerarious fellows; hypocritical old men & ardent youth don't dare draw near: when the time is right, this wise mother leads her daughter by the hand to the kind groom that she has destined for her. He alone has the privilege to engage her: she can never listen to anyone but him. And me: sad object of guilty desires, I saw the audacious crime, the frightening crime, ready to wrest from me the only good thing I had left! Poor Fanchette! Alas! Am I not rather to be pitied, dear Agathe?"

Such were the reflections going on in the beautiful Florangis' head on the day following that fatal day of trouble & alarms, as she folded up & put away the dress that looked so fine on her; & clutching her pretty slippers, she put away the box of jewels that her lover had given her. And her young companion, Agathe, while crying, gave her a thousand kisses.

After Fanchette had removed these objects from before her eyes, her governess arrived. This good woman profited from the first moment of freedom that came along, to run to her ward.

"Ah! Nanny," said the amiable Florangis, "who would have thought! I was so happy in the morning yesterday! I had found so much pleasure seeing myself all dressed up! I did it for Lussanville, who wasn't going to see me anyways, but who is always present in my thoughts; & it didn't take long before these gifts that are so dear to me, from the man I adore, became witnesses to my shame."

"My dear child," responded her nanny while caressing her arm, & stroking her hair, "I'm still shuddering. Lovable girl! What a tragedy! And who would have imagined it! But your lover will come back to Paris: our letters have been posted. He needn't wait two years; barring some new misfortune, I hope to see you both married the moment he returns. He can convince his tutor."

"No, nanny, he won't."

"He must, however: a thousand reasons encourage me to see you united: the news of yesterday's misfortune has gotten around: M. Apatéon does not know what part I play in it; he spoke to me in a way that makes me think he suspects my dear Fanchette was the heroine of that tragic adventure: you were described: you are so beautiful, nobody can mistake you for another; & that charming foot, which everyone considers unique, nobody can get it out of his head; M. Apatéon will have recognized it. I have just warned your mistress: she must not allow anyone to see you, not even women: however, we will make an exception for the young Satinbourg, in view of the service he rendered us yesterday; his eagerness to help, & his zeal, ought to accord him that distinction." Without waiting for Fanchette's response, the governess hastened to depart, to return to the voluptuous old man's house.

"Nanny is being imprudent," Fanchette said, as she watched her leave. "Alas! Does she not realize that all men become temerarious or furious around me?"

"Ah! my friend," said the young Agathe with warmth, "Satinbourg is not like them."

"You don't know them, Agathe, these men."

And the young man paid them a visit. Agathe's presence reassured Fanchette.

"May I, Mademoiselle," said the young fabric merchant, "express all the interest I take in everything that affects you? You should see in me no more than a man who is entirely devoted to you: No, Mademoiselle, not all your suitors are temerarious: there are those in whom you inspire the most profound respect, as well as the strongest affection: such is the man who has the honor of standing before you now. You are the daughter of a fellow merchant; I have offered to return you to the state your parents were in; but if you refuse to be my bride, I dare hope you will allow me to consider you like a cherished sister; & if you will not permit me the first title, I entreat you to grant me the second."

Fanchette was never immune to proper behavior. Satinbourg's behavior touched her. She revealed to him the state her heart was in, & the young man's fervor didn't seem to cool as a result.

"If ever, Mademoiselle," he added, "fate should prevent you from finding happiness with this man, remember then that there is in the world another man who adores you, whose felicity depends only on you." And without insisting any further, he took his leave.

"He really is worthy of esteem, if he's sincere," said the young Agathe.

Fanchette responded to her, "Ah! If you only saw Lussanville! how kind, respectful, faithful, generous he is! & if you knew just how much I owe him!" And the nice girl retraced for her the conduct of her young lover, when he had rescued her from the brutal Financier's lustful hands.

Young people, ah! deign to believe me; this charming sex, unjustly scorned, more than one thinks, is a friend of virtue: for every one Messalina[20] who seeks, by feigned modesty, to give birth to audacity, & who disdains whomsoever is not temerarious, there are a thousand other women whose decent behavior inspire our esteem, & capture our hearts.

Chapter XXVII

Greater danger than anything that's come before.

On receiving the letter from his lover, Lussanville quit Bayonne & with haste took the route to Paris. He traveled night & day; but occupied by the most cheerful ideas, he felt no fatigue. "I'm going to see my divine Florangis again," he told himself each moment. And the name of this beautiful girl, whom he loved, filled him with vigor. Sometimes he takes out Fanchette's portrait; his eyes settle avidly on her face, & seem to be glued to it; they well up with delicious tears; he brings to his mouth his mistress' bracelet of hair: sometimes also his faithful lover's other gift oc-

---

[20] **Messalina: the Roman Emperor Claudius' third wife.**

cupies his attention. "Ah! how everything is precious that comes from the woman one loves!" he exclaimed. "Adorable Fanchette, these jewels embellished you once! Precious tokens, you have carried her, the woman I adore; you have pressed the pretty little foot of my heart's divinity; what voluptuousness it is to touch you! what charms they have! Ah! ah! ah! it is of Fanchette that they partake."

It was in this way that Lussanville passed three days & as many nights on the road. For her part, the beautiful Florangis occupied herself with no other thought than that of her tender lover. Néné stopped by to give her this short letter:

Divine Fanchette, your bridegroom flies to Paris to lay himself before your feet; on the 15th he will see all that he loves in the world.

— DE LUSSANVILLE.

(& it was that same day) when all of a sudden a man appears with a letter for Fanchette & hands it to the fashion merchant: this latter woman gives it to the young Florangis, who cannot hide her joy, recognizing Lussanville's handwriting. He informed her that he was about to arrive, but that a sudden indisposition prevented him from flying to her immediately. He entreated her to come visit him with her nanny. The tender girl was moved, troubled, thinks that his illness is more serious than he lets on, & tears stream down her face. The problem now was how to alert the nanny, who had just gone back to M. Apatéon. The kind Agathe offered to render this service adroitly.

The young girl departs; & in an instant, she returns with the governess, who shared Fanchette's opinion, not to waste a single moment & to go see Lussanville. Florangis appareled herself as she had done on the day of Dolsans' cruel catastrophe; Agathe & the nanny had the foresight to travel by carriage: they climb into it; Fanchette's young friend felt an unbounded desire to accompany them; but she didn't dare propose it; she watched with secret sorrow as the carriage pulled away.

They had only just traversed two streets when a traffic jam stopped them. The coachmen swear, climb down, & go to fisticuffs: in the middle of this commotion, which was enough to make men deaf, an unknown person opens the door to the carriage in which Fanchette sat with her nanny, pulls her out, in spite of the cries they both let out, dashes with her towards a nimble equipage, in which a young man is waiting, puts her in, shuts the door, & in the blink of an eye, the commotion stops, the jam dissipates, the man & the carriage with Fanchette in it disappear.

That despicable abductor was the Marquis de C***. Fanchette, despairing, wants to throw herself out of the carriage, at the risk of being crushed to death under its wheels. The marquis held her back & attempted to assuage her by the most tender discourse: but whatever he said only worsened the suffering of a loyal & passionate lover, whom he tears away from seeing again the man she adores. Soon they are racing through the countryside, & Fanchette finds herself all alone, at the mercy of a man indelicate enough to have perpetrated an abduction. To heighten her terror, the carriage stops in front of a beautiful, vast, isolated house, & they have arrived; reasonings & entreaties are exhausted in vain to encourage Fanchette to climb down out of the carriage; violence is once again resorted to; in the scuffle, one of the beautiful Florangis' slippers fell off her foot, & nobody noticed. She is carried into an apartment of the house, at the farthest remove. There, her astonishment was extreme, as she noticed the very portrait she had given to her lover as a gift, the letter that she had written to him, & the other gift she had wanted him to hold on to. At this first moment of surprise, she thought he himself was going to appear, & this hope had something gratifying about it; but she barely held on to it.

The marquis reappeared: he draws near her with his submissive look, & presenting to her a piece of paper, he begs her to read it. A stroke of lightning would have been less shocking to Fanchette than this funereal document. Her lover *was ceding her to the marquis, & promised him to deceive her by a note written in his own hand to engage her to leave the house, & thereby facilitate her abduction;* he added, *by proof of perfect indifference, that he gave to the marquis the presents she had given to him.* He then spoke to her *of the pleasures he was enjoying with another mistress,* & finished *by exhorting her not to sigh for too long.* The tears shed by the tender Florangis streamed down her beautiful cheeks: "Cruel man!" she said sobbing, "he makes off with my heart, & at the same time he wants to take my innocence away from me! And there they are in a nutshell: men! The only man I thought I could have loved, becomes the worst criminal! O miserable Dolsans! you were less culpable...." Such a rude shock was too much for her vital forces; her head dropped to her breast; the light in her beautiful eyes went out; a pallor filled her pink cheeks... And in this state, she looked even more beautiful than before.

The beautiful Florangis is fussed over & attended to; the cruel men, who were the cause of her suffering, could not stop her tears. It was noticed, while succoring her, that one of her slippers had gone missing. The marquis had his men look for it, but without success. Fanchette reopens her eyes finally, whose touching looks would have moved the most ferocious of men; but when she recognized her abductors, she closes them again sadly, & asks Heaven that it be for good.

What a monster is a man who abandons himself to unbridled passions! O holy severity of our Laws! without you the universe will be nothing more than a place of ambush. The vile Marquis de C*** was concerned lest death had seized his victim. He ordered smelling salts be brought in, & that she be placed on the bed: some women show up to remove Fanchette's clothing.

"Do not hope," said the kind girl to them, "to succeed – as long as I have some strength left to defend myself." And on pronouncing these words, she noticed a room whose door was half-open: without their anticipating what she planned to do, she rushed toward it & succeeded in locking herself in. De C*** orders that the door be broken down: his orders could not be executed immediately; but finally the miserable Fanchette is removed from this last refuge. More violence ensues. Without paying attention to the prayers she makes him in a feeble voice, without being moved by her tears, which he defies with a smile... oh! what vices that cruel smile reveals!... the marquis carries the young Florangis into his apartment, shuts the door behind him with his foot, & everyone else retires.

Chapter XXVIII

New despair.

Fanchette was not alone for long with the marquis. The brute was preparing to satisfy his lust when a frightening sound could be heard coming from the courtyard, where the gate had just been broken in. Guards seize the marquis' domestics; he runs; they nab him; the old governess appears; she calls for her ward; she cries out loudly for her; she jumps out of the carriage; she runs through the apartments. And Fanchette, who has no inkling of the reason behind the tumult she hears, tries to summon her strength, & taking advantage of the freedom that's afforded her, she flees, & hides from her ravishers. She exits the house successfully &, although the night is dark, happens upon the road to Paris. She hadn't taken one hundred steps when she sees two men in the distance, who dismount their horses: they hand the reins to a third man who sheds some light on them with a torch, & they advance on foot towards the house, in order not to be heard. Everything was frightening to Fanchette at this point, & she wanted to turn away, in order not to be seen; but she was walking with difficulty given her delicate feet were bare, & the two men caught sight of her. Imagine their surprise & their joy, on approaching, to recognize the beautiful Florangis, who, for her part, recognizing Satinbourg & his comrade, calls out to them to save her! Satinbourg fell to his knees before the sovereign of his heart.

"Adorable Fanchette," he said tenderly, "you, whom all the universe ought to respect, to adore! It is you who are reduced to fleeing! I can't believe it! I am happy to be able to serve you!" Without losing any more time, the two young men join arms together to make a stretcher, & swifter than the wind with this precious cargo, they regain their horses; Satinbourg takes Fanchette with him on his, & holds her in his arms; the two friends regain Paris, & deposit the young woman at the merchant woman's home.

There, Satinbourg informed Fanchette that a letter from her nanny had instructed him about her misfortune, indicating to him the house in front of which one of her slippers had been discovered.

"I flew," he continued, "in the resolution to save you, or to die trying. Damasville, as touched as I was, wanted to accompany me; & by a happy coincidence, which we could not have dared to hope for, we found you." Fanchette had need of repose: Satinbourg & Damasville, content with seeing her safe at last, took their leave.

"My dear Florangis," said the merchant woman, as soon as they had left, "what a new tragedy! Without M. de Lussanville, who just arrived, & who, by chance, found one of your slippers at the gate of your abductors' vile house, maybe we would never have seen you again."

"Do not stab me in the heart, Madame!" countered Fanchette. "Ah! Here's what takes fortune's cake: Lussanville was the cause of it all! I wish I had never met him! There is no way then to tell an unfaithful man from an honest one! Who would have guessed! He seemed so sincere, so kind!..." At the same moment, with her voice broken by sobs, she recounts to the merchant woman what she had just seen & gone through. Fanchette, suffused with grief, overcome by the perfidy of an ingrateful beau & a fake, had her mistress shedding tears over her for her deplorable fate.

"Lussanville! You betrayed me," she said, "inhuman man, you delivered me into their hands... you, whom I loved, you lead me astray! Ah! I was too weak for you! A girl must never lay bare her breast entirely, no, not to anyone, except her husband. It's a mistake, & Heaven has punished her! O I'm overwhelmed with exhaustion & sorrow! I believed, only a few days ago, to have put destiny's hard knocks behind me & I lose more honor today than I did then, & even more of life; I cease to esteem what I love; the man I thought I would soon marry!" And the young Agathe enters the room: she runs up to her friend, holds her in her arms, covers her with a million kisses, & tells her this:

"My Fanchette, I love you more than anything in the world,... after my mother! You, my charming friend! Ah! It's you! I thought I was going to die for grief. If only I had accompanied you, I would have stabbed those vile men in the arm! If you had seen M. Lussanville's transports! But how come I don't I see him? What happiness! he has snatched you from the hands of those wicked men!"

The unfortunate Florangis sighed deeply: however Agathe's sincere testimonies of most sincere friendship relieved ever so lightly her bitter, heavy grief.

The merchant woman & her daughter put Fanchette to bed: carriages stopped outside the boutique door: the tearful governess, M. Apatéon, &

the Count d'A*** got out of them. Fortunately, the fabric merchant had the prudence, & the presence of mind, to say quietly into Néné's ear: "We have her."

The nanny could barely contain a cry of joy, & made a sign to keep the news secret. Apatéon declaimed long & wide against the century's depraved morals; made inquiries of the merchant woman, how it happened that Fanchette had come to live with her, who had placed her there, &c. She responded:

"In the most honest way possible, Monsieur; & as the most kind, modest, & wise girl ever: I received her from an old lady."

And M. Apatéon exclaimed: "What a shame! Where might I find her at present? And in what condition will I find her?" And on saying this, he made as if to depart.

The Count d'A***, with his eyes fixed to the ground, said aloud, so that everyone could hear him: "The traitorous Marquis de C***! A man must have very little merit to need to resort to such means! What will become of her? There is not a corner of the marquis' house that I didn't go through: I will take my men with me & spend the night looking for her."

When Apatéon & the count had cleared off, Néné flew to her Florangis. At first, she was filled only with joy to see her again. But soon Lussanville's evil, & the effect it was going to have on Fanchette, presented itself to her mind. The sobs nearly suffocated her.

"Ah! Nanny," the kind girl said to her, "who would have guessed that he too was a monster, more dangerous still than all the Apatéons, the Financiers, the Dolsans, & the cruel Marquis in the world?"

"Who... what are you saying, my dear child?"

"Alas, the only man I loved, & whom I still love, maybe..."

"Ah! He was surely worthy of you!"

"Him!"

"Poor Fanchette!"

"Nanny!"

"Alas, he is no longer."

"He is no longer!"

"He died trying to save you."

"He... Huh? what are you saying?"

"Ah! Misfortunate girl! We were fooled! The note you read was not written by Lussanville: a falsifier had imitated his handwriting: the disgraceful marquis himself confessed to it, in returning to M. Apatéon the presents that he had had the shrewdness to have stolen from your lover. Lussanville is dead, in an attempt to exact revenge for the both of you." Fanchette stopped listening to her: she was beside herself with grief, destroyed, annihilated; her soul left her.

"Eh! Why tell her all that now!" exclaimed the young Agathe weeping, "do you want to kill her?"

The kind Florangis fainted & remained unconscious for a long time: it was only with a great deal of effort, & after multiple attempts, that they were able to bring her back to life.

"Dear lover!" she exclaimed, on regaining consciousness; "how guilty I am! Ah, Lussanville! My lover, my groom, you, who reign in my heart, I offended you deeply; I outraged you; it was unjust of me to believe your enemies, & accuse you! There is nothing left for me to do, but die." Bursting into tears, the governess & the sensitive Agathe begged her to moderate her grief.

"Have pity on my old age, my dear child," Néné said to her; "do not poison my last days."

Chapter XXIX

There is a cure for everything.

A story, however sad it may be in itself, always suspends for a short while the listener or teller's own troubled feelings. Néné doubtless was ignorant of this maxim: but she acted as if she had known it.

Fanchette sobbed, & kept silent: Agathe caressed her; & the nanny started to recount what had transpired. "Lussanville was hastening to Paris, my dear child; he was only four leagues away; the marquis, since the time of his proposition to your mistress, in concert with the Count d'A***, was watching our every moves; he discovered that M. de Lussanville was loved: he hired a man to follow him wherever he went, & this wretch informed him of his every step, to the effect that the marquis knew the precise hour & day when M. de Lussanville would arrive in Paris. He knew to wait for him at a certain place along the way, four leagues from Paris; & when it was known that he was passing by, he had him waylaid & surrounded by men in disguise; he stole the presents you had given to him, & even your letters: he ordered them all brought back to the marquis' house, where you were taken, & that Lussanville be delayed for several hours. This wicked man profited by this interval to betake himself to Paris, entice us out of your mistress' house here by a fabricated letter, & capture you as his prey. He pulled it off only too easily, alas!

"You were in the hands of the perfidious marquis, & the time to let Lussanville go had arrived. Diligently, upon release, he made short shrift of tracking down your abductors' whereabouts to the house in the countryside. He had noticed from a distance a number of people hanging around at that place; out of curiosity, while passing by, he cast a glance in the direction of the elegantly-built edifice: he was distracted by some bright, glittering object on the ground; it was the embroidery on the slipper you had dropped. He drew near & picked it up; he recognized it; it made him think; but he continued to fly towards Paris. On arrival, without descending from his post chaise, he ordered that he be brought straight here to you. He found me instead, drowning in my tears, & tracing with trembling hand a letter for M. Satinbourg: I informed him in two words as to what had happened: he was beside himself; he informs me hastily what I have just told you; & that clue he held in his hands becomes a certitude from the moment I assure him that you had left home wearing that present he had made for you. He promises to return soon, goes to find some strongmen to assist him, comes back, & when we mount his carriage, I see M. Apatéon coming. I was no longer thinking; I cried out to him: 'Follow us, Monsieur: someone has made off with Fanchette!' We ride at full tilt; & the Count d'A***, who by chance had heard me, followed us too.

"We arrive: we pound in vain on the gates: we

break them down; I'm the first one to enter the house: I look for you everywhere, but I cannot find you, & I pull my hair out: M. de Lussanville, the hypocrite Apatéon, the count, everyone appears equally interested to want to find you. Wasted eagerness! The marquis himself was surprised: he figured he could deny having seen you: one would have believed him perhaps; but Lussanville found your other slipper, in everyone's presence, in the marquis' apartment. He grows furious:

"'You will answer with your life for this,' M. de Lussanville hurled at him, throwing himself at the marquis, 'if you do not deliver her whom you have shamefully ravished, & whom you hide from us still.' The marquis looks at him with a bitter smile on his face. He acknowledges his infamy, defies Lussanville, admitting his deceitful actions to M. Apatéon, & says in a half-voice to your lover: 'Come fight me for her, this so beautiful girl.' Apatéon alone heard this fatal word, but he didn't anticipate the outcome! The two go off, & one moment later the Count d'A*** cries out that Lussanville has just fallen. We all run: his blood... ah! My dear child! I'm still trembling... his blood soaked the earth red; but the marquis' people (apparently to remove evidence of their master's crime) made them both disappear; we could not find Lussanville's body nor his enemy's anywhere. I'm desperate, I run, I come back: I find M. Apatéon & the count in the marquis' apartment, standing there, calmly reading through the letters that were stolen from Lussanville. That old Tartuffe took your portrait & the other pledges that your lover had received from your hands. He considered your slipper: 'Ah, the little coquette!' he said to the Count d'A***: 'as you can see, she knows all her advantages! She finds nothing more amorous to ornament her foot with, that pretty little foot, which is the most seductive & dainty little...' 'One has to wonder, Monsieur,' I said, 'about these offhand remarks of yours, at a time like this, in this house of horror.' I was indignant, adding, 'The poor child maybe is no longer!...' The old man, composed, turned red in the face, & we both went looking for you. Finally disheartened, overcome with lassitude, we placed guards to stand watch over the marquis' house & people, & we came back here, promising ourselves that we would return the following day.

"Fanchette, what pure joy I would have felt, when I found you here again, if only Lussanville... Alas! dear Fanchette, you're all I have now; & I find you... from the bottom of my heart, I feel a satisfaction... My girl! If you wanted to, I could enjoy a few moments... Moderate those tears, my adorable girl, I beg you, & deign to live for her who has acted like a mother to you. My dear little child, what benefactor's hand led you back to this refuge?"

"Satinbourg & Damasville, nanny."

"Satinbourg! Ah! Tell me, dear child, how, by what happy accident?"

The good Florangis told her nanny all that had passed, & the old Néné blessed one hundred times Heaven, which protects the innocent.

"That poor Satinbourg," she exlaimed, "ah, Fanchette! But I don't say anything yet. My dear, Heaven didn't destine you for Lussanville. Come on, my child, one must submit. Honestly, in life, how many people are more miserable than you? Quite a few. But it's true what they say, there's a remedy for everything in life, outside of death."

"Ah! Nanny, let me cry, let me moan, let me... I've lost everything!"

"Yes, my dear girl; let's both be afflicted together; never has anyone had more legitimate cause."

Chapter XXX

That which consoles afflicted lovers.

"Are you thinking, Madame," said the young Agathe to the nanny Néné, "in lieu of consoling her, after having made her desperate, that you will show her all your sorrow! Hasn't she got enough of her own?"

"Alas! my dear Agathe, she is only too much alive; & I share my own in order to moderate hers."

"Ah! Would that God might assist me to diminish my own like that; at this rate, soon my tender friend will not feel anything anymore!" And they were all three found moaning & devastated on this day.

Satinbourg, uneasy about his beautiful mistress' future, visited the fabric merchant's boutique in the morning; but he didn't dare present himself at Fanchette's door: M. Apatéon & the Count d'A*** returned from the Marquis de C***'s house; & the governess went out to visit Fanchette. She was delighted to find the young fabric merchant there; it was on him that she founded her hopes & Fanchette's consolation, since the loss of Lussanville. She led him herself to the beautiful Florangis' room. The sensitive young man was dismayed by the state in which he found her. He expressed all the goodness of his heart, by shedding sincere tears over his rival's fatal end, which Néné apprised him of.

"Divine Fanchette," he said, "I approve of your regrets, even though they tear my heart to pieces: no, I entreat you, do not take me for the most tender lover any longer, & have no fear that I might demonstrate an indiscreet love for you: you have lost the only man who was worthy of you, I do not believe I will ever be worthy to replace him: I won't pretend to that anymore; but suffer me to let you see other feelings, no less sincere & no less vivid: it is the glorious title of your friend that I pretend to: Beautiful Florangis, you see in me a man who wants to obtain from you nothing but your esteem, who begs you to choose life, if only for another. I have told you, Mademoiselle, you have a brother in Satinbourg: he does not offer you the half of his fortune, which you would refuse, but something more precious: his perfect devotion; a respect that will never be belied; an attachment that will go out of its way to avoid being uncomfortable, & all the feelings that you deserve."

The governess' heart was softened, she threw her arms around Satinbourg's neck & hugged him just like that. Fanchette, totally overwhelmed, completely destroyed, nevertheless felt at the bottom of her heart, stirrings of gratitude, & let the young man know by her eyes that she was touched by his generosity.

That was a lot for a first visit, & at so cruel a moment as this. The governess & Satinbourg understood this; they left the gentle Florangis alone, the one continuing to conceive ideas of consolation, the other nurturing a ray of hope.

"My dear son," said the nanny to Satinbourg,

as they were leaving, "all my hope rests in you; if you can succeed in softening her heart, my girl will be saved... & you are quite worthy of her: honest, tender, faithful, generous, you have just displayed feelings that cannot miss their mark on a soul like Fanchette's. At present, I desire, as much as you do, to see her become your wife: you will be happy together! You see how wise she is, how she makes people love her! Ah, my dear son! Lussanville yesterday lost a possession, more precious than life."

"Do you think someday my love will touch her?" responded the young man, "If only I dared to believe it! Yes, Madame, I swear to you, if I cannot obtain her hand in marriage, my decision is made, I will renounce any other engagement, & I will never live for anyone but her. What happiness that would be however to spend all the moments of the day next to the adorable Florangis! To see her smile at innocent caresses! Yesterday I saw a neighbor who for two years & running is the happy possessor of a young beauty, whom he obtained only after surmounting a thousand obstacles; they were alone; they were chatting, & they said apparently the most tender things to each other: the young bride was seated, her husband standing: he leaned down towards her & stole a kiss; she looked up at him, smiling, with such an attitude on her face! Ah, Madame! There are no words that could describe that enchanting attitude! Her spouse goes in again to kiss her; he renders homage to a thousand charms; successively his burning lips travel across her forehead, her eyes, her nose, her cheeks. She's literally palpitating with pleasure: her half-closed mouth seems to wait with impatience for her beloved's, which comes finally: she wraps her beautiful arms around his neck. That happy state that I witnessed made my heart shiver a thousand times. 'Beautiful Florangis!' I thought to myself! 'Ah, if only I was yours!... more tender still, if that were possible; more... You would be for me more than a bride & a lover, you would be divinity itself.' But I'm getting off track, Madame; & the words escape me, as soon as I want to describe it to you, just how I would cherish, just how I would adore, the beautiful Fanchette."

And the governess found herself in front of M. Apatéon's house. She learns that the devout old man, after having heard Mass, & eaten his fill, had just exited with the Count d'A***. Néné wants to profit by the occasion; she searches the old man's rooms, finds Fanchette's portrait, her pretty shoe, her letters, & takes possession of them all: following her heart only, she wants to give to Satinbourg the presents that were in Lussanville's possession; but the delicate young man asks her to give them first to Mlle. Florangis.

"That I might have these treasures by her consent, & by her hand," he said, "& then I will be happy."

The nanny agreed that he was right, & Satinbourg departed.

The governess put the affairs of the house in hasty order: her every desire was to be near Fanchette: she cherished that charming girl with the same passion that, formerly, she doted on her lovers. It's worth noting in passing that one man's treasure is another man's burden, & familiarity breeds contempt: if one is ignorant of the art of constraining sometimes one's sweet effusions of emotion, love abuses its privileges, & friendship itself nods off. The desire to assist Satinbourg with respect to Fanchette was still a motive that occupied Néné. Lussanville was no longer; & the nanny was quite upset about it; but her grief was not like that of the young Florangis'; she ardently desired to see him replaced, & to see her ward advantageously married. On arriving, she gave her what she had taken from M. Apatéon, & started in on the story that the young merchant had just told her. Fanchette listened to her; but her wound was still bleeding: the desolate lover was unable to begin thinking so soon about forming new bonds. However, without realizing it, the tears she had shed in abundance earlier, now became less bitter, as Néné assured her that another hand was found all ready to dry them.

"Lussanville! My dear Lussanville!" she said, "I have lost you then! No, dear lover, let no one speak about love to me again, nor marriage; I will love nobody but you; I will be faithful to you, even beyond the grave."

And her tears began to flow again. And this state of mind had a somber, but hidden sweetness to it. What could be adulterating it then, with such sincere regrets? Ah, my dear reader, – it was her love for the young Satinbourg! His tender & generous love, which told Fanchette that she was adored, in a manner that befitted her; & which seemed to her as strong maybe as her feelings of loss for Lussanville. Unaware of any of this, the governess acted accordingly: for this good soul never contradicted anyone.

Chapter XXXI

Which will surprise.

Monsieur Apatéon & the Count d'A*** arrived at the Marquis de C***'s house. They found the doors open, the furniture lifted, & the guard posts abandoned: so unexpected a spectacle made the devout Apatéon pause: the Count tries to appear no less surprised: they visit, search, examine: everything has disappeared; whoever was responsible had gone so far as to damage the flowers that decorated the garden. There was nothing else for them to do than to turn around & leave, to ask the guards for a report of their conduct, & have them punished if they were to blame; but those unfortunate men, when found, looked broken, beaten, & half-dead. Apatéon paid a visit then to the Countess de C***, the Marquis' mother who, a former coquette, makes every effort today to repair, by a highly advertised devotion, a conduct that was more than lax previously; but her totally external piety resembles Apatéon's; instead of edifying, she gives rise to new scandals. Apatéon was at first badly received by her: when he mentioned a hideaway, an abducted girl, she was barely listening to him; she told him that she did not know what he was trying to say; but no sooner had he given his name, that famous name in the hypocritical circle of devout persons, it was altogether something else: the old coquette acts surprised; from a corner of her eye she peers at Brother Apatéon's vigorous & predestined attitude, promises to satisfy him as to the marquis, asks him to follow her into the voluptuous boudoir that serves as her Oratory. Such good fortune was not at all what Apatéon was looking for, or expected; but he had to resign himself to it. In the evening, the poor man, very fatigued, returns home, with less hope than ever of finding his pretty ward. As for the Count d'A***, he was more anxious than he let on, & looked for new clarifications.

For many days, the pains he took were fruitless. But while we wait for him to be informed about Fanchette's fate, & for the time when he might let us in on his designs, let's just say that that good girl regains her strength little by little, & meanwhile speaks with the young Agathe about nothing else than her dear Lussanville. One day the governess comes to her with a frightened look.

"My dear girl!" she said to her, "we are ruined: M. Apatéon, who, doubtless, will have read the letter that I wrote to Lussanville, didn't let on to me about it; but he has just discovered that your portrait & the rest of your things were stolen from his house; he is furious: & to make matters worse, he knows, I don't know how, that you reside in Paris: you don't have a choice: either you fall back into his hands, or you marry the kind Satinbourg. He pretends not to suspect me: he has confided in me that he will do everything in his power to get you back again; & if he does not succeed, he will... My dear child, the very thought of it makes me shudder: he will have you reported as a runaway, as a p*** to the authorities; he's a villainous blackguard! I would report him, if he dared do such a thing; but he spoke only in this way to frighten me. Dear Fanchette, make up your mind: give Satinbourg your hand in marriage; he has already informed his mother, to gain her support; she consents to everything. I showed them the document in which your father makes me guardian after his death: the box that contained it, made into the same shape & small size as your mother's foot, when she was your age, struck Madame Satinbourg with strong emotion; she could see her in her mind: in their youth, they were bound together by the most tender friendship; she was privy to her most intimate secrets: she recounted to us how your father, having origin-ally seen that pretty shoe at the shop of the cobbler who was making it, asked for the name of the young woman who was destined to wear it: he found out, saw the beautiful Fanchette Rosin, your mother, then burned with passion for her & resolved to do whatever it took to have her hand in marriage. It was he, your father, who, in order to preserve forever the image of that delicate shoe, had the box crafted per-fectly in its image. 'And that's how he won Mlle. Rosin's heart,' she added: '& her daughter?' 'Ah! Mom,' Satinbourg interrupted her in a lively manner, 'she is even more beautiful: if you could only see hers!' Madame Satinbourg smiled knowingly: she needed no more coaxing. We had your father's last testament looked into: legal *counsel* confirmed that it was sufficient to make your marriage valid, without M. Apatéon's consent. Come with me, my girl, & embrace your future husband. Do you hesitate, Fanchette!? Ah! What misfortunes, my sweet child, you are going to bring on yourself! Come, my dear little child. Your lover would have come with me if I had not dissuaded him; but I didn't want him to be witness to this first moment."

Fanchette, troubled, moved, undecided, wept for Lussanville, & tried to decide on Satinbourg. She had on those slippers, the present from her first lover; the young girl found the act of adorning herself in them to be an inexpressible voluptuousness for her. She gets up & is about to take a step; maybe she was going to accompany her nanny: her eyes were fixed on Lussanville's gift; her heart hardens: she shivers.

"Eh! so it was for another man then, dear lover," she cried, "that you wanted to embellish me! No, no, nanny, I cannot."

"My child, do you want to oppress me?"

"Let him hope, if need be, but it's not yet time to give my hand in marriage."

Try as she may, the governess could not change the beautiful Florangis' mind. The clock was ticking: Satinbourg, anxious after not having seen them appear, feared some accident; he enters the house; he finds the governess at Fanchette's feet, begging her to be persuaded. The young girl hugs her nanny, & begs her to give her a few more days to decide.

"All that Mademoiselle needs," said Satinbourg: "Why mortify her by pressing her so strongly? Adorable Florangis," he continued, "might I at least entertain some sliver of hope?"

Fanchette looked at him dispassionately.

"Eh, well! Any answer will do," he added, "I dare ask a favor: that precious portrait that your nanny returned to you..."

Fanchette lowered her eyes, blushing.

"I don't ask for anything else," exclaimed Satinbourg, "my adorable mistress; I leave my happiness up to you: you will determine my fate; it could not be in a better person's hands."

"I'm embarrassed, Monsieur," responded the kind girl; "to have done so little to merit the feelings you show for me; but I dare assure you, that if there is any method to occupy a second place in my heart, after the memory of Luss***, him whom I consider my husband, the route you are taking is it."

"I am too happy," responded the young man. "Let's go, Madame," he said to the governess, "to bring this response back to my mother; it will make her understand the full price of Mademoiselle's love: & as for us, let's take also all precautions necessary to preserve her from the misfortunes that threaten her." On taking his leave, Satinbourg noticed the young Agathe's eyes were welling with tears.

"Ah, my friend!" she said to Fanchette, "I'm not surprised that you still love so tenderly your dear Lussanville: if M. Satinbourg had been chasing after me, & I had lost him, I would never be able to console myself. Happy is she who will be his wife!"

"My dear Agathe," responded the kind Florangis, "would you love him?"

"No. Because one does not love, when one is without hope."

"But if you could hope?"

"If I could hope? I would prefer M. Satinbourg in a split second – to any man in the entire universe."

("O Heavens!" Fanchette said to herself, "you give me the means to be free, without being hard-hearted or ungrateful. That's it, I have made up my mind.") "Listen to me, Agathe;" she said out loud, "out of gratitude for this young man, out of respect for my nanny, I was going to give myself to him; but he will be happier with you, than marrying me, a girl whose heart is full. If I have any power over Satinbourg... let me tell you what I am thinking..."

The merchant woman showed up & interrupted this conversation, which was followed by what one will see in the next chapter.

Chapter XXXII

How a devout man oppresses the innocent.

"Men surround the house, my dear Fanchette," said the fabric merchant, "& the hypocrite Apatéon leads them. Let's try, my girl, to get ourselves out of this new danger."

The young Florangis gets up immediately from her chair & was about to follow her mistress: Apatéon, escorted by some armed lackeys, presents himself.

"Softly," he said to her, "slowly, my dear child... But do not be afraid. I thank Heaven, which allows me to see you again, & that I might take you again under my wing & lead you along a certain path, far from the ambushes laid by seducers, & sheltered from this corrupt world's dangerous reefs."

"I thank you for your troubles," said Fanchette in a firm tone of voice, "& I exempt you from any further lavishment of kindness on me."

"Ah! ah! my dear girl, don't cop an attitude with me: you have the experience, that you didn't learn here clearly, & of some small adventures boisterous enough to scandalize one's neighbor, which make it a point of duty for me to remove you from... Don't interrupt me, I beseech you. And as I have anticipated that the habit of a free life in this house would make life more agreeable to you than in my house, where a rather bothersome regularity rules; where one is obliged to attend the Offices, to perform good works, to mortify oneself; as I have opined that you could betray some small repugnance to being placed again under my control: to obviate all that, & to do away with a multitude of difficulties, debates, small details, which a spirit of contention & indocility would occasion, which one contracts by frequenting worldly people, by the good character that I'm blessed with, naturally & with assistance from on high, I have fortified myself; not with any spiteful-ness in mind, or that I would have felt necessary; but, as I have made you understand, to do in the quickest manner possible what is in your best interests, most efficacious for you, least subject to excite in the home trouble & emotion that produce inevitable alterca-tions, little difficulties, & who knows what else: an absolute resistance; I have provisioned myself with an order, in due legal form, by the Magistracy, & I have asked these gentlemen to accompany me, to avoid any trouble; & if some one or more of those in whom your dangerous beauties inspire criminal de-sires should get it into their heads to try & stop me in the pious & charitable work that I'm doing, they would be dissuaded by the fear of God & that of these men. So as you can see, it is futile to delay. You must come with me."

I beg my reader not to be upset with me, if this wicked man's discourse is revolting; such is the language used by all those who cover their injustices by the veil of religion. Apatéon has Fanchette appre-hended in spite of her resistance. The young Agathe holds on to her friend; they cannot be separated.

"Let her, let her," said Apatéon, in a benign tone of voice, overjoyed to snag two girls instead of one: "the good work will be double." The merchant woman is desperate, she cries out that her daughter is being abducted. But nobody pays attention: the officer in charge of the minions is persuaded that she will be better off in M. Apatéon's hands, than in her mother's. A carriage was waiting. The sensual old man climbs into it with Fanchette & her companion.

At this moment, the two strangers of whom I have spoken previously, & who, by chance, were crossing the street where the fashion merchant lives, recognized Monsieur Apatéon & the beautiful Florangis; they want to approach them; but the guards who are at the doors, push them back, & give the signal to depart; they take off at full tilt. The Asiatic gentleman & his son's governor cannot get over their astonishment: they stumbled upon the young beauty whom they had been looking for in vain; they see her with Apatéon, their old friend, surrounded by henchmen, like a prisoner; they look at each other. "Is it a dream?" they ask themselves, "or are we in the land of fairies?"

If particular reasons, that one will learn about someday, hadn't prevented the stranger whom Fanchette's little foot had charmed from visiting acquaintances he knew in Paris, what running around for him, agonies for Néné, & perils for Fanchette could have been avoided!

Be that as it may, the devout Apatéon & the two young beauties he has abducted arrive that evening at a pretty house seven leagues from the capital.

Chapter XXXIII

Crime does not always end in success.

He would have missed his mark entirely if he had unmasked himself immediately. Apatéon, although sure to have been outed by Fanchette, conducted himself in the same manner as if he had hoped to be able to impose on her again.

To start with, he put the two girls in the same room together & took away the key. Then he dismissed his escort; supped soberly on two young partridges, a dozen larks, ortolans, quail paté, filets of sparrow in a salad, two bottles of wine from Bonn; for dessert, composed of excellent compote, & all sorts of confiture, it's said that he celebrated with one bottle of Aï; on leaving the table, he went outside to the vast parterre to inhale the flowers, & to meditate, while digesting his meal, on what he would do with the two girls he had had the adroitness to abduct under the aegis of the law.

Fanchette took it badly; she was furious. Apatéon, having seen the governess' letter to Lussanville, & Fanchette's note, had become sure of two equally important things: that his pupil had kept her cool; & that Néné alone had arranged the young Florangis' escape; but as he was satisfied with his housekeeper's services overall, he resolved not to exact vengeance on her (what a sacrifice for a devout man!) & to be more careful in the future, by hiding his pretty pupil, and by conducting her to that house, unbeknownst to the old governess.

He soon understood that it would be difficult for him to keep Fanchette: he was not unaware of all the previous assaults made on the tender girl's virtue;

& her stubborn resistance augmented her charms in this lustful & devout man's eyes. He had his two young friends served sumptuously at mealtime; allowed them to take walks in the garden; affected much gentleness & good-naturedness; except for the first night, always ate with them in the same room. If Fanchette had remained in the dark as to his real character, she would have been the crafty old man's dupe. By the second day, he had all her finery brought to her; & to ensure that she wore it, he had the clothes she was wearing at the time of her abduction removed. He took the same measures & acted similarly with Agathe; several days passed without any change in Apatéon's comportment or in their situation.

The amiable Florangis' state of mind remained unscathed: she promised herself that the old man would gain nothing from her in this ruseful way, & gave similar counsels to the young Agathe. On the other hand, the memory of her dear Lussanville occupied her thoughts: she was not upset with having been removed, at least for a small while, from Satinbourg's importunity, & those also of her nanny. Everything, even setbacks, work to the advantage of true lovers. The young Agathe poured out her soul & her heart's secrets to her bosom friend. "I wish to God," Agathe said to her sometimes, without realizing that she was tearing Fanchette's soul apart, "that you could still be with your dear Lussanville, & that I might have touched Satinbourg's heart!" The beautiful Florangis looked at her innocent & naïve friend, & with her eyes filled with tears she smiled at her ingenuousness.

Nevertheless, the tranquillity that they enjoyed was a brief one. One evening, as they were taking some fresh air in the garden, they noticed the white & red glare of fireworks that had been launched in the courtyard. Curious, as all young women are, Fanchette & the vivacious Agathe ran to the balcony to enjoy more at their leisure the unexpected spectacle. But as soon as Fanchette puts her foot upon it, the balcony collapses: she lets out a piercing cry; Agathe, in despair, rushes after her friend but stops in the nick of time: Apatéon was right behind her; he held her back, & places her in the hands of his men, who take her away....

Not too long thereafter, Apatéon returns to Fanchette's young companion in her room: he kids himself into believing that he could repair the affront he had just pulled off: he assumes an afflicted attitude, sighs heavily, & says: "Kind Agathe! alas! your friend is no more: her fall was equally fatal for the three of us; I will never be able to console myself. I loved her so fondly! Heaven is my witness: I sought only to lead her along a path to salvation, & my fondest desire was to see her happy. Ah! why did I snatch her away from the place she had chosen for her home! Miserable!..." It was in this way that he sought to insinuate himself into the young girl's heart, after having left Fanchette, whom he had had escorted by his men to a secret apartment. Agathe's despair was too vehement to moderate. "Vile monster," she responded, "it is you who killed her! you... She told me all about you, wicked man! I will make these walls echo with my cries. I want to be free! Let me go to my friend, whom I will cry over, & moisten with my tears, rather than live with a man such as yourself, a hypocrite & an abominable monster!" Apatéon tried caressing her in vain; nothing could moderate her affliction; she pulled her hair out, she beat her breast, black & blue, & slapped her face. The old man, seeing that she really did want to die, for the first time felt some remorse; he had just committed a pointless infamy: his hard soul was moved. He calls his men; he has Agathe bound; & perceiving that his presence was irritating her more & more, he left her alone.

Meanwhile, as this vile hypocrite feels only ill-humor instead of the sensual pleasures he had hoped to enjoy in his hideaway, behind closed doors, with his beautiful young prey, – the governess, Satinbourg, & the merchant woman are in utter despair. They torment themselves in vain to try & discover the path that Apatéon had taken. The merchant woman runs to the magistrates; Fanchette's nanny tries to extract information from domestics at the house in Paris; & Satinbourg goes into the countryside searching for clues.

Chapter XXXIV

What is not useless.

Let's get back to our unknown lover, the Asiatic stranger, who had found himself a witness to two striking scenes involving Fanchette; Lussanville's prompt departure for Bayonne didn't help matters any for him: it had deprived him of clarifications he had hoped to obtain; for instance, where she hailed from, & who her parents were, &c.; many other means were available to him to gather information, but he doubted their efficacity.

Chance, – that vague word, putative father of events one knows nothing about, – as chance would have it, on the day after Apatéon's abduction of Fanchette, the Asiatic man found himself paying a visit to the Financier, Lussanville's uncle. While looking for papers he wanted to show him, he opened the box holding the young Florangis' cute slipper. The Financier had gotten too good a look at it previously not to recognize it immediately. He expressed his surprise; & the Asiatic, who recalled that the young beauty, when he saw her the first time, had just left this same man's home, spoke to him about the woman he loved.

"She would appear to be a charming girl," said the Financier in response to his questions; "but she is a prude & a sot: & she has a mania for virtue; she's all in on the sentiment bit. However, for all her beautiful attitudes & grimaces, it cost Lussanville his life, my poor nephew, who was crazy about her."

"What exactly are you telling me, Monsieur?"

"An annoying story, very annoying, because even though my nephew was an imbecile, who, well, – blood is thicker than water, right? & what can I do? The family of his enemy holds the power in their hands; finally, would anything I could say or do bring him back to life?"

It is impossible to describe what was going on in the soul of the stranger during this discourse: an animated, pure joy, never felt before, & a sweet hope filled his heart; he felt as if he were nineteen years old again; he asked more questions of the Financier who caught him up on a thousand things all of which redounded to Fanchette's credit & honor.

"She lost her lover," the Asiatic mused, "I will see about repairing that misfortune: I will dry the tears streaming down her cheeks: what bliss, to find a virtuous & beautiful girl in my fatherland!"

Having been sufficiently informed by the Financier, he departed & went to find his son's tutor, to have him join him when he paid a visit to the young Florangis' mistress.

The merchant woman, after having taken ineffectual steps to recover her daughter & Fanchette, went home again, distraught. She was soon visited by a representative of M. Apatéon who came to inform her that M. Apatéon was a saintly man, who did not abduct girls, except as to ensure their honor. The fabric merchant had good reasons not to believe a word of it; she began to disclose the devout individual's conduct: but the subaltern officer to whom she made her appeal, after having made her understand that he was not there to hear calumny & baseless accusations attributed to a respected & rich man, took his leave, without giving her the least sliver of hope of ever seeing her daughter, or Fanchette, again.

It is at this instant of grieving disappointment that the Asiatic man presented himself, to gather more information about the girl he had resolved to make his companion in life. The good fashion merchant was not in the mood to satisfy him: she had no doubt in her mind that he was just another suitor, as dangerous for Fanchette as all the others: she dismisses him & his friend abruptly, without telling them anything. The unknown lover was no more surprised by this reception than by all the rest he had received: he would encounter difficulties, where naturally he should not expect to find them. The reasons preventing him from seeing his old acquaintances after his arrival in Paris subsisted; but he resolved to pay a visit to M. Apatéon: Néné was away when he arrived, taking care of some unfortunate business matter that had cropped up; he found only the new domestic whom the devout man had left behind: this young man knew absolutely nothing about anything, & could not answer any of his questions. The Asiatic learned diddly-squat about anything that had to do with Fanchette's last abduction, or about Apatéon's mysterious behavior; but he was beginning to see that the beauty of the girl he adored put her sometimes in regrettable situations.

The reflections he made on this subject, the meager success he had had for the many troubles he had given himself to find his son again, & the rest of his family, strengthened his resolve more than ever to devote himself entirely to Fanchette: she was the only person who could repair his losses, by joining together with him; but first he had to find her.

One day when he had left his quarters to catch a bit of fresh air outside the city, in his reveries he walked down a crossroad by chance: he had gone farther than he thought; it was getting late when he realized that he was lost: a pretty house caught his eye; he approached it to ask directions: two men came outside, who, not noticing him at first, conversed out loud together. "D'A*** will lead us," said one of the two, "he will pry her away from that rascal Apatéon. It would be, in all honesty, too bad if that old Tartuffe enjoyed so beautiful a triumph...." At the name of Apatéon, the Asiatic started: he would have liked to learn more; but he found himself so close to them that they noticed him finally. He asked them to indicate to him the shortest path by which he could return home. De C*** (for it was the Marquis himself), seeing a man of good appearance, told him that it was getting quite late; that he was now two leagues away from Paris; & suddenly he invited him into his house. "You will be surprised," said the obliging young man, "by the poor state in which I find myself here: the apartments haven't been set up yet; we live on the ground floor." They walk down into a large hall, well lit, sumptuously furnished: he who appeared to be the master of the house invited him to sit down at the table; he had such a polite manner, was so frank, so open, that the Asiatic stranger couldn't refuse, besides which he would have other reasons for accepting the invitation; for he hoped to learn something about his mistress. But nobody said a thing about what he so ardently desired to know. On getting up from the table, the stranger was led to a small, extremely proper suite of rooms, where everything exuded the Marquis' good taste: the paintings on the walls, the furniture, nothing that didn't smack of luxurious voluptuousness. He spent the night there.

On the following day, the stranger was thinking to return home: his young host made all kinds of attempts to have him stay. He found enjoyment in the Marquis' manners: he found him generous, obliging, honest, & agreeable company... And there you have it, in a nutshell, how men are constructed: just & fair in all that does not touch on their favorite passion, they believe they can redeem their misbehavior, & merit the title of an honest gentleman, by practicing virtues that don't annoy their vices; but they are wicked villains as soon as it is a question of their cherished penchant. The marquis was a kind, galant, delicious, & dishonest man, – the stranger was enchanted by him.

It was not difficult for him to notice, now that he found himself inside one of those agreeable hideaways where Bacchus & Cypris held sway alternately: his mores were not the most rigid in the world; he was one of these men who ran after pleasure & who are always satisfied with themselves once they have found it: he saw women there who sold them-selves; young flanks of flesh that were for sale; girls who had been abused, deceived, seduced; he profited by all of it; but he was always hoping during the course of his stay there to learn something about the object of his love.

Chapter XXXV

Strange covenant.

If the most ardent zeal, & the most avid friendship, do not prevent us from taking false steps, O God! what misdeeds & misadventures will lukewarm conductors lead us to! what horrors will voluptuous, avaricious, corrupted mothers not be guilty of!

One morning the Count d'A*** paid a visit to Néné. "I know where M. Apatéon is keeping her," he said; "I can point it out to you, & take Fanchette off his hands; but you do realize how ridiculous it would be for a man like me to act in this way only for your little Satinbourg: the young Florangis is too beautiful for someone to oblige her without personal interest. You do understand what I'm saying. I will not get in the way of him marrying her: it can be arranged such that he will be no less happy. Think about it. Apatéon has her securely locked up; & without me, I doubt that you might ever see her again. I will tell you more, but I need your consent to abduct Fanchette; I am loathe to be involved in a situation similar to what the Marquis de C*** found himself in: as a general rule, I want only what is given to me: I put all my hope on the power you have over your ward's mind & behavior: it will be easy for you to make her see that in life there are circumstances when one gives up a part in order to save the whole. I will give you one day to decide: tomorrow at this same time, I will come to know your mind." He leaves when he is done speaking. And who was quite embarrassed? It was the governess.

"My dear Fanchette!" she said crying, "what a fatal present Heaven has given to you, by making you so beautiful! That said, Apatéon will take what we refuse to give to the Count, & that, with no other recompense than her grief. What must I think, unhappy me! And there are all these cruel men! They are foresworn & perfidious, or they will sell us their services at the price of what is most precious to us. I have met only one man in my life who was worthy of being a friend; & he was the one I was led to deceive. Ah! if I should agree to his terms, the tender Florangis, more virtuous still than she is beautiful, would prefer death to dishonor." Agitated by a thousand different thoughts, Néné stepped outside, to go & consult with Satinbourg himself, & with him to take measures to mollify the count, to try to pique his generosity, or prevent the effect of his bad designs. She didn't find him in. She was told he had gone out riding the day before; & the poor governess, disconsolate, her mind riddled with fear, her soul weighed down by sorrow, found herself in an even greater state of embarrassment.

The count did not fail to appear the following day at the designated hour: he presses the nanny to make up her mind; he makes her grow anxious of unexpected misfortunes awaiting Fanchette. He reminds her above all that it is only by politeness & consideration that he asks for her consent to enjoy Mlle. Florangis' favors. And to prove to her that he knows exactly where she is & how to get at her, he shows her one of her pretty slippers, assuring her that he came into its possession while Fanchette was sleeping. Seeing the slipper, hearing his story, the governess makes up her mind.

"As much as it depends on me," she said, breaking down, "I promise. But swear to me on your honor that you will act with discretion at every step of the way." The count committed himself by a thousand oaths. And we have no reason to believe that they were not given sincerely.

Chapter XXXVI

Dangerous assistance.

"Nothing can stop me now," said the count completely beside himself, as he embraced the old Néné. "We will leave this very evening, & tomorrow at the same hour, the tender Florangis will be in your arms, while you prepare her to pass into mine." This last expectation was not at all flattering for the governess: her tears began to flow again more abundantly than ever.

Where did we leave off with young Agathe: she was beside herself, groaning, bound, locked up by herself, in a dark room, on Apatéon's order. She was desperate: "My dear Fanchette," she said to herself, "my lovely, my unique friend, we are now separated forever...." And as delirium took hold of her imagination, which was too vividly impressed, for she was young yet, she thought she could see her, wanted to embrace her, & shouted out to her: "Wait for me, my

Fanchette, wait, I will follow you; I will go down with you into the abyss... Ah! Fanchette! you fall without me. I will follow you. I will follow you in spite of these cruel men who hold me back, tied to this bed, & in spite of myself." So violent a state of mind soon exhausted all the strength of a young, delicate girl: she slipped into a complete exhaustion that was similar to death. It was then that Apatéon dared to approach her again.

Any other man would have shuddered to see Agathe again in the state she was in. For the vile Apatéon, – a man who had grown accustomed to playing God himself, to braving the laws of the land & of Heaven, to deceiving men; a man whose soul had gotten to a point of utter, incurable depravity – for him, it was just the opposite: her despair & her grief seemed to attract & arouse him even more, like adding spice to a meal. But let's tear away the veil & let the reader know only that Heaven did not entirely abandon innocence. No, it does not allow that to happen.

Everyone says so: love & vengeance will find the objects that excite them, even if they are located at the center of the earth. Satinbourg, without guides, without clues, arrives, after three days of searching, at the house of the hypocrite Apatéon. Harassed, unable to go on, he looked at it, without however recognizing that it was the object of his pursuits. He wants to ask for information: he knocks at the door, bangs on the walls, shouts: "anyone home?" No response; he thinks it is uninhabited & is about to leave; but before he does, he walks around it, curious. He climbs up a small butte, & in the distance, on the edge of a casement window, the young man espies something that looks like a woman's shoe. He does not yet know what it is; only he presumes that someone lives in that solitary hideout. It was difficult for him to get closer to the object he had seen: the window looked out over a narrow garden that was surrounded by walls taller than the rest of the enclosing walls. He tries again to have someone open up for him, but without success; & suspicions are born in the back of his mind. Daylight was diminishing: as soon as night allowed him to scale the wall without being seen, Satinbourg grimps up, jumps down into the narrow garden, & goes straight to the casement window: he reaches it by means of an espalier, & he takes possession of what he had seen. Imagine his surprise on discovering that it is one of his lover's slippers, which Lussanville had made a present to her of! He no longer doubts that this house belongs to Apatéon. He renews his efforts to arrive at the window; but in vain: besides, it was protected by vertical bars that would have prevented him from climbing in. He had no idea what to do next, when he heard some activity outside the house. He fears someone has discovered him & hightails it without rescuing Fanchette: he scrambles up the wall again, in the reverse direction, exits the garden, & approaches with precaution another place, to understand what made the noise he heard earlier; he sees two post chaises, horses, & armed men, who seem to be waiting for orders: the Count d'A***'s voice strikes his ear; he recognizes it perfectly, but he has the prudence not to make himself seen. His soul was stirred by a thousand different thoughts; he wondered: "What is the Count doing here?" He wasn't in doubt for long.

As soon as d'A*** had given the signal by striking his hands three times, all his men approached the house. Satinbourg, without being detected, joins their ranks. In an eye blink, the doors are opened; they enter, & the young fabric merchant, guided by what he had seen earlier, seeks to penetrate the apartment where a casement window looks out over a small garden.

Fortunately, Satinbourg had not seen the governess, whom d'A*** had brought with him: for not knowing how dangerous the count's efforts were for him personally, he would have probably made himself known sooner or later. From where he stood, d'A***, seeing that everything was going according to plan, & that he was finally going to be master of the beautiful Fanchette, approached old Néné. "Ah, my nanny," he said to her, "any moment now you will see your dear ward: remember our convenant; it would be too dangerous for you, & for her, to want to play me... At this price, I give her her freedom: she will marry Satinbourg when she sees fit: I will keep my promises & my oaths; but you, gadzooks! be faithful to yours. After this exhortation, unfortunately too energetic, the count gave Fanchette's slipper back to the governess. "I'm giving this to you in exchange for something much more precious to me," he said to her. "Tell that beautiful child that the man who saved her wants to press her hand, see her portrait, & have all the other presents that Lussanville possessed; that in addition he waits with impatience for the gift she must give to him, when he holds her tightly in his arms, & he whispers into her ears, all the while gazing down at her... pretty little foot." Then the count took Néné by the hand, & led her quietly to a secret corridor; all the doors had been opened for him by a traitor in M. Apatéon's service, who had decided to deceive his master, for his master wanted to instill the fear of God in others, but then dupe them effectively.

The distraught governess followed her guide, trembling. "What have I promised?" she thought to herself, "& how despairing Fanchette will be! The poor child will want to die rather...." They arrive at the door of the most distant room; but Heaven! what a surprise for the count! there's no one inside! the man who led them there was speechless. They search, they look; it was only after one hour that they noticed that two of the bars protecting the casement window were moveable: the young Florangis had escaped by it; & how did she do it?

Chapter XXXVII

When the dead come back to life.

Apatéon, in the middle of the silence of the night, tormented by the demon of lust, found himself lying next to the young Agathe, bound tightly to the bed: he dared, with sacrilegious hand, to touch that sweet temple of purest virtue, & timid innocence. Suddenly, a dull sound is heard: he shivers; & the coward, believing that it must be thieves, trembles, but for his life alone. His terror redoubles a moment later when someone approaches: a tumult of men attack the door of the room where his penchant for young flanks, & a certain crime, had just led him. The door is broken down: Agathe is taken from him, & from this room of horror.

The Count d'A*** & the good Néné, at first surprised that Fanchette was missing, suspected Apatéon had brought her to the room where Agathe was held, whose despair was painted in most graphic details by the traitorous domestic; they run there, just in time for the fabric merchant's daughter, who remains in full possession of her virtue. After having delivered her from evil, the count places her into the governess' hands. That dear girl thought she had gained a new lease on life, on seeing her dear Fanchette's nanny again; but soon, recalling the cruel accident that had befallen her friend, she abandoned herself once more to grief, & recounted amidst sobs to the old Néné the beautiful Florangis' tragedy. "She lives, my dear Agathe," the governess told her; "it was a trick by the cruel Apatéon to separate you, as we have just been informed: a machine makes the balcony fall & rise, very quickly, making you believe there's an abyss: but Fanchette, alas... should I be afflicted or overjoyed? She is no less lost than before: nobody knows where to find her."

Agathe's eyes remained wide open, which by birth were fairly large already, & one could see painted on her face an embarrassment, a happy perplexity, that is felt when one comes to doubt an irreparable misfortune. "Was I awake, or was I dreaming?" she thought to herself.

"Yes, my child," said Néné, "we have just learned that the fireworks set off were done expressly to attract you two to the balcony: the accident that separated you was carefully planned; Fanchette got off unscathed, except for fear; but they wanted to take away from you all hope of seeing her again. Apatéon thought he could take advantage of the state of abandonment you found yourself in. Eh! who knows whether she will have been able, like you, to come away unscathed! we have no idea what's become of her, & by whose hand she's been abducted." Agathe had no idea what to think or feel: "Abducted, from an abductor!" And the good Néne wept bitter tears.

The count, sure that the beautiful Florangis was no longer at Apatéon's hideaway, came back to the governess & Agathe, who at this moment were in the room that Fanchette had occupied. He brought with him a young man by the hand, whom my reader does not know: the count himself didn't know him either: the governess remembered having seen him before; but, being occupied with Fanchette, nothing else interested her: one will learn his secret when the time comes.[21] "I have not found the person I was looking for," he said: "& here is a man whom I never imagined finding here; but Fanchette cannot be far: let's hurry."

Néné said to herself: "O God! please see to it that my good girl is in good hands: bring her back safely to her governess; I will no longer be bound to the count in that case, & as of tomorrow she will marry Satinbourg!"

Heaven fulfilled only half of her prayer. The count departed, taking with him the young Agathe & old Néné. Apatéon began to recover a bit from his fright & considered himself all too fortunate that his precious self had not been manhandled; finally he is encouraged, grows bolder, misses the beautiful Florangis & her young friend, collects his frightened domestics, & dreams of vengeance. And my readers will be surprised hence to learn whom the hypocrite exonerates & whom his fury will be unleashed on.

He arranged to return to the capital, to blacken innocence; he was meditating on the means by which to deceive again the magistrature & make them oppress his pupil, when he received a letter from the

---

[21] a young man: it is doubtful that the reader will remember. Would he happen to be the Asiatic stranger's long lost son?

new domestic he had left in Paris: this man informed him that a man, who said he was an acquaintance of his, had come several times to visit him. This man gave his name. The devout man turned pale, & exclaimed: "Oh Heavens!, what a setback! I thought he was dead!" This news determined his next steps; he deferred his departure for Paris by several days; & when he returned finally to the capital, it was in secret: for all anyone knew, he was still in the country. But let's leave this wicked man, a prey to fears & remorse, to meditate on new crimes to cover the old ones, & let's return to the kind, touching, & beautiful Florangis.

Not far from that famous bourg, where the beautiful Estrées welcomed into her arms the best & last of the HENRIES,[22] the young Satinbourg, with the delicate Fanchette riding on the back of his horse, was forced to travel on foot, holding the reins of his horse. The tender girl, overcome by fatigue, could no longer support it & was ready to pass out. He was provisioned with some refreshments: he offers them to the sovereign queen of his soul. "Beautiful Florangis," he said to her, "it's a friendly hand that offers these to you; take a deep breath at last: you are with a man who adores you, but whose respect equals his love; who, ready to immolate himself for you, wants nothing more than to serve you, the pleasure of being useful to you, & the certitude of seeing you happy."

"Monsieur," Fanchette interrupted him matter of factly, "you have just proven that to me."

The day was beginning to get into full swing:

---

[22] Estrées...: a village and commune in Aisne, France, from which hailed, presumably, Gabrielle d'Estrées, who in the 1590s became one of King Henry IV of France's most important and influential mistresses.

the tender Florangis was barely able to speak these last words, which, in spite of his concern for her weakness, made Satinbourg's face shine with joy, when they noticed a band of men riding straight for them. Soon they recognized the Count d'A***. Satinbourg felt a twinge of anxiety: Fanchette shuddered; but when they saw Agathe & the governess among them, they felt reassured & straightened up even as they came before them. The young Agathe jumped out of the carriage & ran to her friend; old Néné followed suit. All three embraced & hugged each other; but the governess inundated her dear Fanchette with tears; Satinbourg watched with satisfaction; & the Count d'A*** was thinking about the promise the nanny had made.

The sight of Fanchette aroused his desires: in her rich habits, which Apatéon had earlier embellished her with, her charms took on a new brilliance; her air of dejection & a sweet languor made her a thousand times more fetching; her foot was warm in that pretty white shoe that had inspired such intense desires in the lascivious Apatéon, when she used to play the harpsichord; *Venus* & the *Graces* would have envied her charming slipper; the Count's eyes were fixed on Fanchette's pretty little foot, always the prime mover of her conquests, misfortunes, & deliverance. The delays made him suffer: he called out it was time to depart & placed the object of his criminal desires alone in his post chaise, with her nanny: by placing this last person there, he meant for her to arrange to speak with Fanchette & to keep her word. To start with, he wanted Fanchette's portrait, & the other jewels so dear to Lussanville; he said as much in a tone of voice that indicated he wouldn't brook no for an answer. The beautiful Florangis was in tears when she had to part with so many of these things, which had become more precious to her since they had been in the hands of her lover. The young Agathe & Satinbourg sat in the other post chaise. The count, mounted on a superb white steed, pranced around Fanchette's post chaise. All the rest of the cortege was on horseback: they took off, & after they had marched for a while, it was remarked that the count had veered them away from the route towards Paris.

"Alas, it's over," thought the governess to herself; "we will not escape this last peril, in which I myself have precipitated the dear Fanchette." And with her eyes welling with tears, she was about to explain the terrible secret, when Satinbourg cried out with a loud voice: "Count, where are you taking us? Aren't you also no better than a vile ravisher? Listen up: Mademoiselle Florangis would deserve a crown, if only for her virtue & beauty: I recognize that your rank places you above me: if you love her, & if you pretend to possess her in a legitimate way, her happiness is far more dear to me than my own, & I allow her to ride in your carriage... But if, now listen up, if things should happen to go any further than that, it will be over my dead body." The Count d'A*** could not contain his rage; he dismounted: the two rivals drew near to one another: the count keeps back his men, who wanted to overwhelm Satinbourg. "Leave him be," he said to them, "& do not dishonor me by wanting to serve me: my own arm suffices." Trembling, completely beside themselves, Fanchette, her nanny, & the young Agathe rushed between the two combatants to separate them. The count wouldn't listen to anything they said; he was going to run Satinbourg through with his sword, but Agathe held him in her arms. Several unknown men ran up; one of them, with an awful beard & his hair disheveled, was unrecognizable; he yelled out: "Stop, perfidious man, & tremble!" At this moment, another person, the young man whom the count had found at Apatéon's hideaway, moves into the field of battle: he runs to the count's adversary: "Ah, my friend, my long-lost friend!" he bursts out, wishing to embrace him!... The terrible stranger, who does not stand down, pushes the young man away; &, throwing himself at d'A***, the two men begin to fight with a fury. The stranger's men put the count's men to flight; the ladies climb back into the post chaises, expecting the worst; & Satinbourg, seeing that his liberator has the upper hand, hastens, at the behest of Fanchette herself, to lead them down the road to Paris... Alas, she was following, & who would have believed it! the man she adored now. And as they made their way to Paris, the beautiful Florangis was growing further apart, without realizing it, from her dear Lussanville.

Chapter XXXVIII

Calm follows the tempest.

Agathe & Fanchette were received at the merchant woman's place with inexpressible transports of emotion: the governess felt uneasy; she was cursing the customs & laws of the land, which didn't allow her to lead Fanchette & Satinbourg immediately to the altar in order to unite them in matrimony. "Stop making things more difficult, my dear child," she said to her; "your delays have very nearly ruined us." The kind & tender Florangis looked at Agathe & smiled: "Have no fear," she said. And the good Néné took this for consent. After caresses & celebrations, the fashion merchant made the observation that the testimony of two girls would not suffice to unmask Apatéon; that doing so would merely dishonor themselves, in a country where the men of *gilt* are always right. (She could have added, *& pretty women*; but maybe she knew that a young beauty, to restore her reputation in a brilliant manner & prove her virtue, must begin by losing it many times with a *** & a *** & even sometimes with a ***; whatever the case, she didn't bring up the bit about pretty women.) She spoke of the visit paid by two strangers, who asked questions about Fanchette; communicated her fears to the governess, & concluded that the young Florangis should go secretly into a convent, unbeknownst to everyone but the governess & Satinbourg, which she would not exit until her wedding day. To avoid new reversals, this resolution was executed immediately; the young Agathe begged her mother not to separate them: so the two of them were escorted to the convent B*** on rue V*** by the merchant woman & her governess, who prescribed the behavior that must be followed with respect to those who might ask to speak with the pretty recluses.

From the moment the two friends were alone, they exchanged stories of what had happened since their separation. At the picture the young Agathe painted of her frightening despair, the tender Florangis broke down in tears. Then the merchant woman's daughter spoke of the perfidious Apatéon's attempt on her virtue, & she told her how, when she was without strength, without movement, & almost dead, as she was about to become the victim of his brutality, the count, the governess, & their men came to her aid. Fanchette in turn told her story: "when the balcony collapsed, my dear," she said to the young Agathe, "I passed out for fright: I came to again in the arms of those who were carrying me, with Apatéon in the lead. I closed my eyes, suspecting some deception on the part of this monster: they placed me on a couch; everyone exited, & he alone remained with me. My dear little Agathe, that abominable man, more wicked still than I had ever imagined, imagining me unable to defend myself, he... I had soon recovered my courage, & taking possession of his hunting knife, I threatened to plunge it into his unworthy, loathsome heart, if he dared come near me. He exited, mumbling something about you. I spent the rest of the day & night in the most intense sorrow. Overcome still with sorrow the next morning, in a state where I was more dead than alive, I felt my eyes grow heavy; I fell asleep. When I awoke, it was one o'clock in the afternoon: I discovered someone had taken one of my slippers; I shuddered. 'Who could it have been,' I asked myself, 'if not Apatéon?' The vile man would have profited by my sleep, which was perfectly natural for him, to approach me and... These reflections gave me mortal anxieties that my nanny alone, when I confided them in her, knew how to calm. She also told me that it was not he, but the count, who, with the aid of a domestic, reached me. I never saw Apatéon again: Heaven inspired in me the idea of placing on the ledge of the casement window of my room the other slipper I had. If someone among those who might be searching for me noticed it, by this clue, I told myself, they would know where I was: it was a present given to me by my dear Lussanville, who had already saved me. I still had hope. I wasn't disappointed: in the middle of the night & during all the tumult, I hear a banging on my door. 'Beautiful Florangis,' the voice said, "is that you?' I respond, this someone enters, & I see Satinbourg, who shows me what had guided him to me. I felt I could trust in this esteemed young man: 'It will be dangerous for us to go back the way I came,' he told me; 'let me see if that window will allow us to escape.' I don't know how he did it; but he had soon shaken loose two bars; he made me go down first, with the assistance of a rope ladder; he follows me; he looks for the garden gate: the one he finds opens onto the countryside; his horse was waiting for us; we departed. You know the rest, my dear Agathe." And the two friends caressed each other again, as if that moment had been the first since their escape from peril.

Far away from the tumult of abductions & ravishments, Fanchette, who had been transported all of a sudden to the calm of monasteries, thought she had found in these houses of religion a picture of the bliss that is promised to the Elect. "Ah!, my dear Agathe," she said to her companion, "how charming this place is! & why didn't my nanny place me here earlier, when I was delivered out of the hands of the Marquis de C***?" The young Agathe was as surprised as Fanchette was, & rested her head on her shoulder.

Sister Rose, a young professed sister, eighteen years old, with a lily-white complexion, an elegant waist, & whose heart was still more tender than she was beautiful... Sister Rose had been charged from the first day of the their arrival by the Mother Superior of the convent to keep these two new boarders company. "How happy you all are, my Sister!" said Fanchette to her, after they had had several conversations together. "Here you rest at port. This corrupt world, which soils, in spite of itself, the purest of innocence, has no more power over you. Alas!" she added, looking at Agathe, "my dear little one, I think it is here where Heaven calls me to stay: Satinbourg, if he wishes to trust me, will find happiness by attaching himself to you: & me, occupied in my thoughts by the lover I lost, I will spend, in this salutary retreat, the rest of my life, whose most beautiful days have been spent too often obscured by the clouds of misfortune."

"No!" cried out Agathe, "no! I never want to be separated from you; you are more dear to me than all the world."

Sister Rose sighed; & letting fall a look of pity on the beautiful Florangis & her innocent companion, she said: "You have no idea just how much you would complain," she said to them, "if, like us, unable to escape, you were confined to this place that appears so tranquil to you now. Young imprudent girls! don't be seduced by it! We thought so too, like you, when not having been engaged, everything our eyes saw, in the monastery, was seen through rose-colored glasses. However, I would never have decided on my own to lock myself up here: hatred, ambition, an unjust preference in my unnatural mother decided my location & vocation here... But there's no point in my going on about my misfortunes."

"Alas!" Fanchette responded, "I'm not the only unhappy person here then! Sister, if it is not too much to ask... Ah! Tell us what made you shed those tears that were streaming down your face just now, kind, tender Sister! Agathe & I, we can find solace in each others' disappointments: you, above all, inspire in me a desire... I don't know how to express it: I feel such a great sweetness in letting myself go with you. Please don't say no...."

"I consent," replied Sister Rose. "Having just now piqued your curiosity, it is only right that I should satisfy it."

Part Three

Chapter XXXIX

New characters.

"They call me *Rose* in here: on the outside I'm called Adélaïde. Although not of high rank, my parents were rich; they had three children; my older brother, my younger sister, & me. From birth, I had the misfortune of displeasing my mother. As soon as I outgrew my wet nurse, I entered the convent, where I stayed until fifteen years old. A fatal accident had taken my father away from me: & love, which caused it, seemed thereby to give the signal for all the ills that were then in store for me. My mother's imperious character had alienated her spouse from the first days of their marriage: exigence is love's poison; & my father having felt an emptiness in his heart, wanted to fill it. Made to please, he didn't take long to find what he was looking for: another woman, whose extreme beauty attracted a bevy of lovers, captivated him; he gave utterance to his feelings, & they were reciprocated. But this passion, equally criminal for the two of them (for he was attracted to a woman who, like himself, was bound by sacred vows to another person), could have only dire consequences. Loved, preferred, he was fooled by appearances; he thought he had been betrayed by the woman he adored, the only woman he cherished: he wrote to her a reproachful letter, & attacked his rival; blinded by rage, his pistol discharges in vain; he receives the fatal leaden slug in his belly.... His mistress ran to him; it was too late: but he recognized her still; she convinced him of her innocence; he died in her arms, his mind occupied only with her & her sorrow. After his tragic end, that unfortunate woman did nothing but languish.

"On my father's death, I was called home. The time I spent there was filled with so many mortifications that I can no longer remember all that I suffered, without feeling for an unjust mother all the hatred her inhuman behavior merited. I lived to cherish my brother; I was not envious of him; I felt what must have been the weakness a mother had for her son, on whom she placed her greatest hopes; besides, this dear brother softened the odiousness that my mother's preference for him could have made me feel for him, by demonstrating an affection & a tenderness for me that were never belied. As for my sister Bibi, I have to admit that I didn't have the same feelings for her: she was younger than me; her face & her character had nothing to recommend itself to me: there was nothing but a blind prejudice for my mother, which made her prefer her to me. Added to which, my sister, priding herself on the attentions that should have been shared equally among us by our mother, looked on me like a stranger in our paternal home.

"Such was my predicament when my mother became particularly fond of a neighbor, who, under the guise of devotion, led a life of sensuality & excess. It was this wretched man who exacerbated my misfortune. I had the ill fortune of displeasing Monsieur Apatéon (that was his name)."

Fanchette & the young Agathe gasped.

"Do you know him?" asked the kind nun.

"Alas! Yes," said Fanchette, "& it is in order to hide myself from his persecutions that I'm here: but continue," she added, "we will fill you in later, when you are done telling your story."

"I was young, lacking in experience," resumed Sister Rose, "this seducer, before I thought to distrust his dubious maxims, had subjugated my mind without my realizing it, blinding me as to my true duties. At the same time, a person worthy of my attention offered me his heart. He was a kind young man, the son of a rich merchant of *Pondicherry*, who had sent him first to France, where he himself hoped to return in good time, if death hadn't taken him. As for birth & fortune, he was my equal: but it was love that really bound us together. He was introduced to the family by my brother, whose friend he was. Although I was always pestered, either by my mother, or by the devout man who never left her alone, sometimes my lover found the occasion to speak with me alone: he knew how to please me, to persuade me; by the time of our second conversation together, he obtained my permission to inform my mother of his wishes. Unfortunately for us, he chose a moment when Apatéon was by her side. Several times this vicious man sharply interrupted my suitor; & as soon as he found himself alone with my mother, he had the meanness & inhumanity to take advantage of the hatred he noticed she had for me, in order to satisfy himself at my innocence's expense: he convinced her that this young man, being rich & independent, was a favorable candidate for my younger sister, whose sublime qualities he exalted. Monsieur Apatéon's advice appeared marvelous to my mother: but, also on his advice, I was to be kept in the dark about it.

"Meanwhile, this wicked man, as soon as he found himself alone with me, never stopped telling me about the pains he was taking to convince my mother to consent to my marriage with the young

Valincourt (that's my suitor's name)."

And he is also, dear reader, the young man found recently locked up in the devout Apatéon's house in the country, where apparently he had him go for a retreat, for the salvation of his soul: he is also the Asiatic man's son, sought for in vain, & who will be reunited with his father when they least expect it.

"He called me his dear daughter & held me in his arms. Me, who considered him my protector, my friend, & who also didn't understand the subtlety of all that; I resisted him but little. Far from moved by my innocence, he saw only the opportunity to triumph by it, & he applied all his attention & energy henceforth to find the right occasion for his designs.

"My mother was too impatient to follow M. Apatéon's counsels to the letter: she liked so much the advice he had given her, of offering her youngest daughter's hand, instead of mine, to Valincourt, & of employing a stratagem that would engage him in a way he could not back out of, that she could not resolve to follow all the expedients & delays he was prescribing. She wanted to get on with it quickly. One morning, having learned that my lover had just arrived, although she was still in bed, she had him introduced into her apartment; Bibi, after having received word from my mother to get dressed & pay her a visit, although nonchalant & without much interest in it, made short shrift of her toilette with my assistance because I thought she needed some help: she exited the room brilliant enough to make a conquest. While I, far from seeing her as a rival, was giving her all the factitious charms of an elegant appearance, my mother was lavishing on Valincourt the most tender caresses. He didn't know what to think,

& it didn't take long for him to imagine that she was infatuated with him, she whom he was preparing to call mother. He was quickly disabused, when he heard her call him her dear son. This so sweet name, & which he desired so fervently to live up to, softened him to the point where tears of joy were seen to well up in his eyes, & he held my mother in his arms. A young girl's steps were soon heard: the room was dimly lit: Bibi passes along the ruelle: 'Here is my daughter whom I give to you, my dear son,' said my mother to Valincourt, while placing his hand in Bibi's. My lover could not detect the dark & bizarre deception that was being played on him; he mistook my sister for me, & kissed her hand a thousand times.

"'May it please God,' exclaimed my mother, 'that this very moment should see the consummation of a union that would make my & my daughter's happiness!'

"These words instilled a certain boldness into Valincourt's soul. What can I tell you, my charming companions? He was head over heals in love with me: he thought he was rushing into my arms, there on the bed, beside a mother (whose judgment clearly had been perverted by Heaven). My sister, Bibi, didn't say no. My mother put up with everything.

"My lover, beside himself with love & joy, knocked himself out with testimonies of gratitude; when the light of day, coming in through the windows, showed him his error; he was petrified, confused. Without giving him enough time to regain his composure, my mother, impudently (it must be said), praised the rare treasure he had just made himself the master of: she talked up her dear little girl, in comparison to, she said, I was nothing but an imbecile, an idiot, obdurate & opinionated, a coquette, surly, capricious, who would make a husband miserable. Indignantly duped, Valincourt was enraged. But what had just happened made him circumspect; he had the prudence to dissimulate. On leaving the house, he adroitly made me understand that he was going into the garden. I went there without affectation. It was then that he told me, with tears in his eyes, everything I could learn about that incident. He promised to be faithful to me until death did us part.

"'It was you I swore my oath to,' he said: 'it's you who were given to me: instead of fooling me, your mother & sister fooled themselves, cruelly.'

"He wept. I wept with him: for, knowing my mother's hatred, I predicted an onslaught of persecutions. Valincourt reassured me; & to protect me from the bad treatment I anticipated, he consented to feign a kindness & an obliging attitude towards my sister, while I waited for him to reveal a project to me on which both our happinesses depended.

"Before letting me in on his plan, Valincourt wanted to see what would follow from his earlier intimacy with Bibi in my mother's apartment. He reaffirmed his vows to me, more strongly then ever, after having assured himself that he had nothing to fear from any of them. It was then that, by a note he handed me himself, he caught me up on everything. I shuddered with horror & jealousy: my mother appeared more unjust to me than ever; my sister became odious to me. My lover read in my eyes all that was going on in my heart & in my feelings: but we were never left alone to talk about it; he could not speak openly with me; chance favored us finally: I approached a casement window, & he came to join me.

"'Dear Adélaïde,' he said to me, 'if you wish, I would like to marry you....' He was going to walk away after uttering these few words, but noticing that my mother had just passed into her room with Monsieur Apatéon, & that my sister was playing with her little pooch, which yielded to the caresses of another dog, its lover, that the benign Apatéon himself had complaisantly brought with him, he continued: 'All that's needed now is a bit of resolve, & a lot of love. The governor who stands in for the kind father I have lost, approves of my passion; he thinks of you in the same way I do; together, we have arranged that he will oppose my marriage to Bibi: your mother, whom I informed of the good old man's dispositions, was hoping to counter them by what you know; she can no longer count on it; she is inconsolable about what might make another person's joy, & I am sure that it's only a matter of time before I find myself again with Bibi in the same situation. It's our turn to deceive them. Do you love me enough to be up for that'

"'As for love,' I said to him, 'you already know how I feel about you: it's merely a matter of resolve; I have very little of it: my mother scares me to death.'

"He didn't respond, because my younger sister drew near.

"The following day, he returned at a very early hour: he penetrated the house as far as the room I occupied with Bibi, without being noticed. I had already gotten up.

"'My dear Adélaïde,' he said to me in a soft voice, to avoid waking my sister up, 'come hear my vows in the arms of your mother: don't be afraid: I've arranged everything...' & without giving me any time to respond, he exited. My heart was beating: I didn't know what to do. But finally love took the ascendant over my timidity. I entered my mother's apartment; a perfect obscurity reigned there: Valincourt walks up to me; he holds me tightly in his arms. Apatéon had many times before told me that one must never refuse the person who truly loves us. I was quite sure that Valincourt loved me in this same way. What I didn't know was who loved whom more.

"Keeping my wits about me, I felt him at my knees: 'Adorable Bibi,' he said to me, loud enough for my mother to hear him, who pretended to be asleep, 'I'm the happiest man alive, an insurmountable obstacle separates me from your sister, while the most sacred bond, the double chain of pleasure & love, binds me forever to you.' I didn't quite understand what he meant by all that, but finally he said in a soft voice in my ear that he swore he would marry me, & I was satisfied.

"I left him. On returning to my room, I found my sister Bibi who was just waking up: she looks at the hour, gets a move on, & I noticed that she went to my mother's apartment, where my lover was still. The sight of it made me wince, without knowing why. But Valincourt had removed all my anxiety, by exiting immediately after she came in.

"It seemed as though love, given I had abandoned my heart to it, wanted to favor us: several days later, my mother leaves the house in Monsieur Apatéon's company: the devout man appeared at first to have wanted to profit by her absence, to speak with me; he gave her his hand begrudgingly: my sister accompanied them on the way out. Valincourt who was thinking only of me, seized this precious opportunity.

It was the first time he had seen me since our earlier adventure & his triumph. He explained to me how he had played his hand, when my sister appeared, in a way so as to be able to impose upon my mother. At that moment, our eyes crossed: in Valincourt's eyes was a burning desire: mine, I cannot deny it, responded in the same fashion; he stole a kiss; I was loved: I agreed to everything; how could I be upset? My lover, attentive not to displease me, observes his progress: he sees my moist mouth form into a sweet smile; it was all he needed... In my arms, he got drunk on those delicious pleasures that he disdained having partook of with Bibi.

"We were no less happy the following day; they left me alone again; Valincourt returned: he acted in the same way as the day before... My dear friends, the following day, & the day after that... for an entire week, – the memory of it fills my mind with heartrending regret, – we enjoyed the sweetest pleasures together in each others' arms. One day (it was the first day of my misfortunes), I waited for my lover: my mother & Bibi had exited; he does not come. A note, delivered to me by a trusted hand, informs me that we cannot meet. Instead, I see M. Apatéon appear. I respected him: I knew he was there on purpose, to try to help me support my lover's absence.

"'Your mother & your sister are faraway from here: it's the eighth or tenth trip I've had them make, & the first I wanted to profit by, to avoid their suspecting anything. We need to chat, you & I, & to converse freely how to assure your marriage with the young Valincourt. I can help speed it along.' What an idiot I am! I thanked him! He interrupted me: 'Everything depends on you, beautiful Adélaïde; if only I can count on your renewed vigor.'

"'Ah! you can count on it,' I interrupted him vigorously, 'I will never stop respecting you like a second father to me.'

"He told me what he pretended to have done for me: I listened to him with a satisfied air: he slipped his arm around my waist: I smiled at his caresses like a young girl to her cherished father. How far I was from suspecting anything was amiss! My friends, the traitor dared to profane the sacred title I had given him, & once his adroitness turned into violence, he made me unworthy of my Valincourt.

"Imagine just how innocent I was at this time! I didn't even realize I had been violated! Naively on the following day I recounted to my lover how M. Apatéon, profiting by my mother's absence, had excited my confidence in order to gain the upper hand; how he showed his true colors; how I was indignant by his boldness, & wished to gather all my strength to oppose him, but found myself weak in comparison, & I lost... consciousness. Valincourt who was listening to me now, without stirring, kept his eyes glued to the floor. Tears streamed down his cheeks; on two occasions, I saw him ready to rush into my arms, & then recoil with horror. Finally, without uttering a single word, he leaves me, & I found myself feeling frightened by the signs he had given me of a most frightening despair... Alas! the following day, I received this fateful letter from him, which made me wake up too late:

Since the infamous person who dishonors you, & outrages me, is the only person to blame, why did you tell me, imprudent

Adélaïde? Heaven punishes us by an involuntary crime; it tears us apart: I will avenge you & perish for it. Live, my dear & unfortunate lover, whom too much innocence has made a criminal!

"Apatéon entered the room just as I was reading this note; he reads it, turns pale, exits, hastens away, & two hours later, I learn that my lover is dead.

"I won't try to describe for you how I felt, my rage, my despair: I wanted to die.

"I was still in this frightful state of mind, when Apatéon had the impudence to propose keeping alive a criminal commerce with me. I responded to him with all the indignation that he merited. This wicked man then menaced me: he swore that he would ruin me. He kept his word only too well.

"When I had removed all his hope of seducing me, he wasted no time at all by informing my mother, that two girls would diminish her son's fortune by too much, & that she should consider making one of her daughters a nun. He knew my repugnance for that miserable life; he had no doubt also that the choice would fall on me. In effect, my mother, embittered by Valincourt's tragedy & by her fears for her dear daughter (which were however baseless), became more cruel in my regards. She immediately told me that I had to return to the convent, & that in one week I would take up the nun's habit. I resorted to entreaties & tears unsuccessfully. She was inexorable. On the evening before my entering the convent, Apatéon, the cruel author of all our ills, made a renewed attempt on my virtue.

"'You are going to make yourself miserable,' he said to me, 'one word, & I can change your fate. I can do that,' he continued (seeing that I was not responding). 'Come reign over my heart, & wallow in pleasures: I possess the knowledge (rather ordinary actually) of how to make them come alive; the art (more difficult) of varying them; & the secret (quite rare) of preventing disgust.' My response: contemptuous silence. He wasn't put off. I told him then, quite frankly, while casting a damning look at him, that not only the convent, but death itself would inspire in me less horror, than the insupportable idea that he could decide my fate.

"I entered this house, my young friends; since then one year as a novice & two years as a professed nun have passed in utter grief. After having been engaged, I found in this sojourn, which appeared so peaceful to me previously, nothing but the painful boredom of its existence, the odious privation of the most innocent pleasures, a sad prison; the disunity among the unfortunate victims that fill it, the petty intrigues, the curious, narrow, active, disdainful minds. I'm not being unjust; I'm not turning my companions' mistakes into a crime; it's the inseparable vice of a state that reason reproves. O you, kind girls, who enjoy still the possession of what I have lost forever, your freedom, – learn from my regrets that they might inform you. Think on my mournful experience; it would be too late when you are instructed by your own.

"Heaven punished an unjust mother: I had just taken my vows when smallpox took hold of Bibi. My mother had a useful practice tested on me, & which for that very reason must have its naysayers; the effect corroborated the views of the able practitioner, who took care of me; but for some days I was thought to be in danger: that was enough to convince my mother to no longer wish to hear another word about inoculating my sister. That pusillanimous feeling of hers proved to be fatal for Bibi, when she was taken unexpectedly by a natural case of smallpox two years later. My mother was unable to survive the idea of losing that dear idol of hers. She passed away soon thereafter.

"All I had left, I thought, was my brother, his friendship, his tenderness; the frequent visits he paid me consoled me: but for several days I no longer saw him. His governor came yesterday: apparently he has been suffering from some great setback or sorrow. I tremble to think this cherished brother of mine could have, at this moment maybe, fallen victim to misfortunes, which I fear, & which I am in the dark about."

Chapter XL

Wherein one finds nothing that one expected.

Fanchette & her pretty companion thanked the young nun for her advice, promising to profit by it. They told her in turn their story of Apatéon's latest dark deeds; &, as they were speaking, someone came to tell them that a young man & the old Néné were asking to see the beautiful Florangis & her dear Agathe in the parlor.

"Everything is ready, my dear child," said her governess: "we have the consent, the special permission: I have been named your guardian; nobody knows anything about M. Apatéon; we only spoke about your uncle: Come, I will not rest until I see you married to this lovable young man."

Satinbourg took his turn speaking: "I am so happy, if you might be, Mademoiselle: deign to make it happen; for the first time, I dare to pressure you. I would despair however if you felt compelled: beautiful Fanchette, if you preferred to wait another few days, I would accept that, rather than wish to mortify you. I am content to see you safe in this house, the foremost of my desires is fulfilled."

"Nanny," said Fanchette visibly touched, "I would like to speak with M. Satinbourg for a moment in private." Agathe & the governess stepped away & began speaking with Sister Rose. Their conversation centered around M. Apatéon.

"How's that! Madame, you know him as well?" said the good Néné. "Would you believe that I was impressed with him until the time when Mademoiselle Florangis stayed with him? That man has two completely opposite faces: for those whom he has no interest in duping, he is consistently an honest man, conducts himself with decency & devotion to the last scruple; he's quite different from other hypocrites, who rarely go to so such lengths to appear so honest, gratuitously. For those whom he wants to catch in his nets, he changes almost imperceptibly over time, like the needle of a clock moving across its face: before a girl knows to distrust him, he's already succeeded in making her mistake black for white, & up for down; he knows the art of making her blind to things: he prevents her from noticing that he's changed her manner of thinking. For me, who constantly found myself in the first category of dupes, because my advanced age ruled out being included in the second, I commented to myself a number times that for a devout man he ate too delicate morsels of food, that he possessed too voluptuous furniture, that he slept in too late, that his sermons had sometimes a little too much of the opera & comedy about them: but when these thoughts occurred to me, at a certain point I had to brush them aside, recalling that one must not too easily criticize the conduct of one's superiors, who may have secret motives that make them innocent."

"Alas," said Sister Rose, sighing deeply, "that's exactly how he operated on me: I understood, when it was too late, everything you've just mentioned: I was too ignorant: having been raised in the monastery, I had no knowledge of crime & virtue other than by name: he read into my heart; he found no prejudices there to combat: he profited by that discovery, to instill in me a morality that he said was natural. A lover whom I adored profited by it: Apatéon himself. If only I had known what a girl must fear of men's attempts, he..."

"They won't fool me," the young Agathe interrupted them, "& I have learned a lesson from Apatéon's viciousness; he inspires in me a distrust (that can never been too exaggerated) for all men."

The conversation between the beautiful Florangis & Satinbourg had just ended: this latter person had a pensive, dreamy, undecided air about him; his gaze was fixed on Agathe: Fanchette's look was animated, a strong sense of satisfaction lit up her face, which tempered the sadness that had overcome her since the loss of Lussanville.

"Everything has been decided between us, nanny," she said to her governess; "Monsieur has just given me the greatest proof I could desire of his attachment: we will bring it to conclusion tomorrow."

Néné could not contain her joy: she was expressing the most tender expressions of it to her pretty pupil, when someone entered the room to tell Sister Rose that the governor of her brother was asking to speak with her in another parlor.

While she was rushing out of the room, Satinbourg, before taking leave of Fanchette & her companion, informed them that he had just taken possession of Monsieur Delaunage's business. And his eyes continued to remain fixed on the young Agathe, whom the tender Florangis was caressing: he sighed. The governess told him that there was no time to lose; & the two of them took their leave.

Chapter XLI

Wherein one finds what one did not expect.

"I'm overjoyed by the future I have prepared for you, my dear Agathe, if you should wish to diminish my suffering: I find almost as much pleasure loving you as Lussanville made me feel. Dear child! Satinbourg & you, you are perfect for one another: he could never make me happy, because there is no longer a man in the world that I can love; no, not even Satinbourg himself. Your inclinations for this virtuous young man will make him experience a much sweeter fate: he will be cherished by you; you will love him as he deserves to be loved. Because, my friend, I am not blind to his merit; he has quite a lot of it, & I do him as much justice as you do. But I was in love with Lussanville: this passion is so dear to me, that I cannot resolve to sacrifice myself for anyone else." It was in this way that the beautiful Florangis broached the subject to the young Agathe, as they were leaving the parlor, as they returned to their rooms.

When they had returned to their rooms, Fanchette continued: "I want to tell you, my dear child, just what Satinbourg & I talked about. You know how my nanny is: this esteemed woman loves me to excess; when she trembles, she trembles only for me, & when she thinks, she thinks only about the dangers she must exposes herself to while serving me: she wanted to see me safe; I feel safe here: but I have come up with a plan to deliver her from her obliging self-sacrifices, & to make your happiness, at one & the same time. When I was sure that you could no longer hear us, I began my conversation with Monsieur Satinbourg with these words: 'You want me to be happy, Monsieur, I know; & I am suffused with the most intense gratitude to you for your generous attentions: you also wish to secure for yourself your own happiness: what do you think is the most sure & efficacious way to do that?' And I stopped to listen. Satinbourg looked at me, taken aback. I pressured him to respond. 'To obtain you as a wife,' he said to me finally; 'to love you, to adore you...' 'Monsieur,' I said to him, 'you are dear to me; I'm pleased to say so. Now, what I am about to say to you will sound bizarre; but I declare to you in advance that the most tender friendship, a perfect esteem, & all the feelings that you should wish to receive from me have compelled me to it. You are mistaken if you think by marrying me you will find happiness: isn't it true that in your wife, only love, an intense, undivided love, just like you feel finally for me, – only love is able to satisfy you? Will you answer me?' 'I agree, Mademoiselle,' he said. 'Well then,' I contin-ued, 'I can show you all the heartfelt feelings you de-serve, except for that last one: love. But I know someone else, a young person, who is charming, vir-tuous, tender, & who can think of nobody else in the world but you, who is worthy of her attachment. Such are the feelings that you inspire in the touching Agathe, my kind companion. She's quite dear to me, you know: if you want to, you can make her happy; I assure you I'll be as happy as she will be, & because of you. So generous a soul such as your own, Mon-sieur, will not be insensible to these reasonings: Agathe loves you; I can never love another man; her & your happiness are as precious to me as my own tranquillity. That's all I have to say.' 'Ah! Mademois-elle, who would have expected this! Can you...' 'One more thing,' I added, '– don't breathe a word about any of this to my nanny, that you will be Agathe's spouse, to spare us both a thousand little mortifica-tions.' What can I tell you, my only friend? He brought up some difficulties: I shot them down; I said I needed this token of his attachment to me: I got all I asked for, & Satinbourg at this moment is informing his mother about this plan. You should have no doubt in your mind that he will succeed: his mother esteems the lovable young man, & she will be delighted to have you for a daughter. What happiness for me, dear Agathe! I will make no more vows, once I see you married to your lover, & I will be able to tell myself I give to your mother a son to make up for Dolsans."

The young Agathe, moved, serious, was in Fanchette's arms during all this time; she looked up at her with delicious tears in her eyes; she was about to speak when Sister Rose entered the room, express-ing signs of the most intense joy.

"My brother," she told them, "this dear brother whom I cherish..." "Yes, &?" said the tender Fanchette. "Having escaped a thousand dangers... this very evening, or tomorrow at the latest, I can finally see him again! Conceive for yourselves, my friends, what a loss this was when a brother, the one person in the world who took an interest in the destiny of an unfortunate person... They wanted to keep it a secret from me the danger he was exposed to these last few days, all the more so given they had doubts of being able to free him. They were right; I would have succumbed to this last stroke of bad luck; whereas today, hearing it all, even his misfortunes, it increases my joy knowing he will be here again to see me. Ah! share in my joy, my friends; my brother is worthy of all women's interest; he's the most faithful & tender of lovers: to all the charms of his face, he adds every talent & virtue. What a joy for the woman he loves! It's on her account that he's suffered so much, & it's she who will be his reward! What a beautiful end, – I so wish for it!"

"And the woman he loves is she worthy of him?" asked the young Agathe.

"I never met her," responded Sister Rose: "my brother's governor says she's beautiful & kind."

The call for to Vespers sounded: Sister Rose left them then, & the two young friends continued to converse. "I don't know about you," said the beautiful Florangis; "but this young Sister Rose really interests me: I find in her looks... I can't quite put my finger on it. Clearly I'm mistaken: an image too dear to me finds resemblances in things that only exist in my imagination. But let's talk about you, my child...."

"My adorable friend," said the tender Agathe,

"accept a token of gratitude from a heart that is filled with unknown, delicious, & inexpressible feelings; I feel it palpitating in me: a warmth, a pleasure... I'm babbling, dear Fanchette, but in this very babbling of mine you can glimpse my gratitude."

Chapter XLII

Which ought to explain a good many things.

"Where am I, & what did I just hear! in this underground chamber, a voice... My insides are all tied up in knots. I think I recognize my son's voice. Heaven! cries!... the clinking of swords! I shiver: my hair is standing on end: my heart is seized by fright..."

And the Asiatic man, whom we had left in the house of the Marquis de C***, jumps out of bed. He no longer knows what to think of the young man whose flattering welcome seduced him. He wants to leave: he realizes that it's pointless to try, & his distress augments. While disturbed by a thousand thoughts, he chides himself for his imprudence, & his surprise redoubles: an unknown person speaks these words:

"Fear the punishment that multiple crimes merit! Vile crimes! your honor depends on the man you have cowardly oppressed, respecting whom you have shamelessly violated the rights of citizens & humanity! Let me have him, perfidious men: hurry it up... O my son! dear object of my troubles, Heaven permits me to serve you... What do I see here!... & you also, Monsieur! you whom all the world gave up for dead! O unfortunate lover! whom Lussanville & I, we so often wept for!"

At the name of Lussanville, which he just heard, the Asiatic man's surprise stopped: he understood that it was the young Lussanville's governor, Kathégètes, who was speaking, in the act of rescuing his ward. He waited impatiently for the moment to hear what interested him most.

Meanwhile, the old Kathégètes, after having heaped his reproaches on the Marquis de C*** & the Count d'A***, hastens to release his ward & Valincourt from these detested haunts. And this was the morning of the very same day when the good Néné believed that Fanchette would wed Satinbourg, when this latter young man was going to marry Agathe in fact; when Sister Rose was waiting for her brother to appear. The kind Lussanville, as soon as he had escaped the underground chamber, rushes to the side of his governor, & says to him: "Ah, my father! what has happened to the adorable Florangis? Leave the Count & Marquis to their remorse: tell me about my lover."

"Let's get out of here first," responded the respectable old man; "We will have plenty of time to get you caught up, later."

"How were you able to find me?" asked Lussanville as they were making their way home.

"Heaven, my dear child," responded the old man, "uses all the means in its power to save the innocent & punish the guilty. When I was looking for your lover at the Marquis' house, & you disappeared at the drop of a hat; I was surprised by this; but I didn't believe you were dead. I ran to seek a warrant for your enemy's arrest. Despite all the credit he has, yesterday the orders were issued & expedited to me. But while I was rousing friends of your family, I was apprised of your encounter with the Count d'A***; I found myself in a new pickle: what had become of you? For several days, my efforts to find you proved useless. My anxiety increased. I had always suspected the Marquis, although since the abduction of Mademoiselle Florangis, the Count & he appeared to have fallen out with each other. As I was returning to the city yesterday evening, I noticed that men were fixing up a neighboring house of the Marquis'. I drew near, & discovering a garden that appeared beautiful to me, I entered it: an absolute solitude reigned everywhere. I reach charming copses; I enter labyrinths & paths carpeted with greenery; places that would have been delicious if they hadn't been soiled by debauchery. I hear some animated voices speaking in the distance. I proceed with caution, & when the only thing separating me from those who were talking was a hedge of lilacs, I pushed several branches aside & saw the master of the house with two strangers.

"'If one can judge by this portrait & the smallness of this shoe, that's her,' he said. 'She sure is pretty!'

"'When the Count d'A*** displayed this portrait taken at the Baroness de V***'s place,' a young man interrupted, 'all the women said that it was flattering: the Count swore that it was nothing compared to the original: things got worse when he exhibited the pretty girl's shoe; the ladies all cried out in unison; the Count made oaths under his breath: but having gotten it into his head to mention that the baroness' daughter had a foot as cute as the one on display, all those crazy people changed their tune immediately: there wasn't one among them who didn't pretend to be able to put it on, but not a single one of them dared try; everyone, including the young Agnès, her daughter, who had only left the convent eight days earlier, refrained from trying, & blushed.'"

What a feeling of despair for the cherished lover of that belle, when he saw in the hands of strangers those precious gifts belonging to her!

"Imagine my astonishment & the hope I conceived, my dear Lussanville," Kathégètes continued, "when remembering that on our trip back from Bayonne, you held in your hands, for an entire day, a shoe just like the one they were admiring! And my attention redoubled."

"While the young man spoke, the master of the garden examined the portrait curiously, the pretty little shoe, & the box from which it had been drawn. 'Her lover is alive!' he exclaimed with astonishment... 'And does one know who the parents of this girl are?'

"'The beautiful Fanchette is, they say, the fashion merchant's niece, who carries, like her, the family name Florangis.'"

"'Fanchette! Florangis!' the stranger said (I thought I saw him grow pale.)

"'Yes,' repeated the young man, 'she was raised by the same.'

"And the stranger inspected the portrait again.

"'Niece of the fashion merchant!' he said... 'Apatéon abducts her, with orders from the magistrature, obviously, as...'

"'Apatéon is her tutor.'

"'So far as I understand! These traits, that name, the little foot that this shoe suggests... M.

Apatéon's ward... What's become of her?'

"'We'll find out soon enough, but at present we do not know... You sure are interested in her!'

"'A young person I saw one fine day, the person in that portrait, & whose foot this slipper fell off in a singular adventure, inspired the strongest feelings in me, & I resolved to marry her.'

"'Marry her, that's rich!... And yes, that slipper is hers... You've seen her?'

"'In Faubourg Saint-German.'

"'That's where her lover lives, a languorous young fellow, who, like you, wants to wed her, & whom we are holding at my place until either his heart or his mind should be healed.'

"'And for what reason?'

"'For having charmed his mistress: honor, in a nutshell. We will let him go when the time is right.'

"'By what right?'

"'It's not a problem! He's merely a commoner.'

"'I see.'

"'His pretty mistress is a bit surly; we'll send him back supple, inured... If however she was *yours*... we could...'

"The master of the house appeared indignant: he rose without saying a word, & turned towards an old man who had not opened his mouth. They walked towards each other, & exchanged a few words, which the marquis couldn't hear.

"Your lover's shoe made me understand that

the young man in possession of the box that held it was none other than the Marquis de C***; I guessed that you were held hostage at his house. I hastened to withdraw. The marquis & the two strangers gained the house of the former, who had the same attitude of solitude that he wore on his face when he had made you disappear. I expected that this mysterious behavior of his was a cover up for an odious plot. On arriving at your place, I found the warrant for his arrest that I was expecting. I didn't lose a single moment. I found you. You know the rest. But you, my dear son, tell me what happened to you while you were being held by these villains, whom you refuse to avenge yourself on.

"You remember," said the Lussanville, "when the Marquis de C*** provoked me to a fight, & that I followed him. As I was crossing a small courtyard in pursuit, I was going to pull my sword out when all of a sudden I'm staggering; a pistol fires; the ground opens up underneath me; covered by a shower of blood, we drop down into the earth, because we were on a trapdoor covered with grass, & they wanted to persuade the others that we had been wounded. I was led into an underground chamber, where one could barely make things out in the poor light of a sepulchral torch. For several days, I had no idea what had happened to the Marquis de C***. Finally, he reappeared.

"'Your lover is dead, poor soul,' he said to me. A stab of the knife would have been less painful for me. I let out a cry of rage & despair, which the Marquis responded to by long bouts of laughter. 'But before she died,' he continued, 'the Count d'A*** & I, we satisfied on her the desires she inspired in us. With this dreadful news, know that nothing can save you; I've taken precautions to prevent you from ever being found.'

"'And may lightning strike you dead, you shameless bastard!' I exclaimed, 'May it pull down these abominable walls where you keep me, where I am unable to avenge myself!'

"The Marquis de C*** responded with a bitter smile: 'Without your impotent rage, I would only be half-avenged.' He left me. And in his place a girl dressed like a whore was introduced into the room to stay with me.

"The marquis' behavior towards me was bizarre: he went to great lengths to reduce me to despair, by telling me horrible stories, not to mention the death of Mademoiselle Florangis; but at the same time, my table was being served with profuse & delectable dishes of food: he went so far as to want to procure for me those licentious pleasures that are so much to his liking. The dangerous siren that he had placed in the room with me, having tried all her seductive charms on me unsuccessfully, was replaced by another, younger still, prettier, more reserved. At any other time, I could not have been held accountable; but I was lamenting the loss of an adored lover; my heart was shut off from the sweet attractions of lust. I found however some pleasure in speaking with the girl, in whom I inspired the same feelings she was expecting from me. But one must not look a gift horse in the mouth: this reflection proved useful to me more than once as I tried to reaffirm my constancy.

"The passion I excited in this debased soul gave her some moral encouragement, & made her capable of generosity. One day, she said to me: 'I'm happy with you in this prison; but you're not: you're going to be in debt to me for your freedom, you know, the news of your lover, & the opportunity to save her. She's still alive: a certain Apatéon abducted her: the Count d'A*** & the Marquis are planning to wrest her from him; this evening she will come here: the house of old Apatéon is on the route to Burgundy, at several leagues from here; run to her assistance: by way of gratitude, & one day remember me, the both of you.' I was beside myself as she spoke: I embraced the little Lolote, who, without wasting an instant, opened a hidden door in the wall for me to escape through. I found myself in the garden. I hurried to Paris. I counted on finding you there: but you were busy serving me elsewhere. I had myself accompan-ied by all the people of the house & several men they engaged to join me. I waited for the count at a place he had to pass by in order to reach the marquis' house. We stayed put the entire night: morning broke & we began to grow desperate, when I discovered the Count d'A*** at fisticuffs with a young man about to be immolated by his fury. That stranger must have been respectable, given he could take on the count. Followed by our men, I ran towards the more despic-able of the two. I had caught sight of my adorable mistress; but I wanted to avenge her, before showing her the man who adored her. Valincourt came to-wards me; I didn't recognize him: I barely paid him any attention at all: the combat begins, & my friend backs me up: the count's men abandon their master like the cowards they are: I spared his life, because I was the strongest.

"Meanwhile, the young man I had just freed escapes with Fanchette & her nanny. The perfidious count feigns to have been touched by my generosity,

& holds out a hand to me: Valincourt, whom I just began to recognize with the same surprise that you showed me when you saw me, joins him & informs me that he owed him his freedom. I could not turn down this act of generosity. Unsuspectingly, I see the count's men returning. There were a lot more of them this time, & the marquis, whom I didn't notice, was among them. When they got close enough, they jumped me; they grabbed Valincourt; they disarmed us; they led us along; our men were dispersed, & we both get thrown back into the dungeon I was just languishing in.

"The obliging Lolote was gone. All our efforts to free ourselves proved ineffectual. Nonetheless, my situation was much less dreadful than before: I was together with my friend; I told him: the tender Florangis knew their plans; she knew enough to escape their traps.

"Valincourt told me a story then, that I wish I could forget: he recounted to me the misfortunes... the crimes... I shiver still. O daughter of misfortune!"

They were entering Paris when Lussanville stopped speaking. But while he's flying to the fabric merchant's house to find his dear Florangis, or at the very least to find out where she's hiding; while the humiliated marquis turns red in the face before the Asiatic man on account of the affront he just received, & for the generosity of Fanchette's lover; while the stranger & his son's governor quietly applaud the wise government that protects both nobility & commoners equally; let's get back to the convent, where new scenes are being hatched.

Chapter XLIII

Wherein Fanchette's slipper *plays a fine role.*

Zealous as she was to see her ward, the good Néné suffered inordinately for having being unable to quit Monsieur Apatéon's house before nine o'clock. All the emotions inherent in passions, & above all fright, which the unexpected return of the Asiatic man caused in him, had made the devout man fall seriously ill, ever since the beautiful Florangis had been set free: he took to his bed; & none of his domestics' attention came anywhere near to that which, ordinarily, his housekeeper still paid him. From the moment she was free, she ran to be near her dear Fanchette. Her heart beat in anticipation: "I am going to see her married," she said to herself: "my dear girl will have nothing more to fear in an honest man's embrace: I will leave this vicious Apatéon & live with her: I will be the one who cares for her children!" Already maybe her imagination was shifting into overdrive, as it represented five or six children to her. She arrives at the door to the convent, she rings: & Sister Rose, at the same moment, having just left the Choir, comes to visit with the two young boarders.

"Today is the day, my good friends," the young nun said to them on entering the room, "when I will see my brother again. How time drags on in respect to that happy moment! I'm so excited! But I will lose you," she added, while shedding several tears. "You are the only two I could love, after three years, in this place: I would have died of boredom, if my brother hadn't shown up again." And then the governess asks some questions of Fanchette & her companion. "Monsieur Satinbourg is not yet here?" said the old Néné. "No, my nanny." "No! But look at you! Wearing a common dress! With those slippers![23] Eh! my girl! please, go do your toilette at least. On a day like today! It's already enough that one had no time to make preparations; at least you should take advantage of what you've got. Look at Mademoiselle Agathe, how done up she is. But it's all the same to you!" And Fanchette, glancing at Agathe, smiled. And the nanny understood absolutely nothing. Happily, Satinbourg arrived.

My readers should know that the young fabric merchant, having gone with his mother in the morning to visit Agathe's mother's house, learned about Lussanville's escape: at that moment in time, the news of this event had the effect of double the pleasure on him: he was ceding Fanchette; but he would see her happy, – in another man's arms, it's true, but who merited it by all counts: & add to this his beautiful young fiancée, whose love had anticipated his, & who quite allayed the sacrifice. He exited Agathe's mother's house without saying a word, & flew to the convent, in advance of Lussanville's arrival there, in order to engage the nanny & her ward to exit with him before her lover appeared. His purpose was to make her seem even more dear to him by the fear he was running of losing her, on learning that she had left the convent for the altar. Satinbourg, after having brushed aside several small reproaches, & having received many caresses from the governess, begged her to let him speak in private with Fanchette for just a

---

[23] Original footnote: Dear readers, and my very dear female readers, Fanchette on this day was wearing, for the sixth or seventh time, those celebrated, very cute, brilliant, embroidered slippers; the gift that friendship made to love, & love for Fanchette, on the day when Lussanville saved her from being suffocated to say very least by the brutal Financier, & when, the Asiatic man, who was more delicate, could not resist removing one of them (of her previous pair) from her foot.

moment. "I must tell you what I have done, Mademoiselle," he told her. "Yesterday, after I quit you, the desire to oblige you (how many new motives have just been redoubled) made me set everything in motion to become, as soon as today, Agathe's husband: I went to find my mother; I got her caught up on our conversation, & I obtained her consent: I won her over with a bit more difficulty than before; she loves you already: your mother her friend of hers; she had been flattered by the hope of calling you her daughter; but she renounces that hope now only so as not to disoblige you. On leaving my mother, I ran to my curate; the good man has never seen you before, nor the tender Agathe Florangis: by a small finesse, that good intentions make excusable, I had Agathe's name substituted for yours as the name of baptism: the notary drew up the civil marriage contract this morning; the only thing missing is your friend's signature: let's go & visit her mother's house, that my lovable bride whom I receive from your hands might fulfill this formality before her mother. From there we will go to the altar. I see, Mademoiselle, at this moment, clearer than ever, that you could never have been mine; I swear to you at the same time that, after you, there is no other woman in the world who could be dearer to me than your young friend." Fanchette demonstrated her gratitude in the most flattering of terms, which her nanny heard, but didn't understand a word of; Fanchette asked him to wait one moment, & then she ran with Agathe to go hug Sister Rose goodbye.

Fanchette said to this young nun: "Alas! both of us are losing our dear Agathe today; because, as for me, from today forward, I must return here to be with you." And Sister Rose, unmoving, looked at her without responding. Her eyes looked her up & down.

"Heaven!" she exclaimed finally, "it could very well be! Mademoiselle, endulge me here... Yes, I recognize them: that's the embroidery my brother asked me to make for him: that's *my* work... on your shoes. Dear Florangis, tell me, where did you get those slippers?" Confused, Fanchette reponded to her, blushing: "From my lover," she said timidly, "whom I adore, from Monsieur de Lussanv..." Rose threw her arms around her & planted a big kiss on her mouth before Fanchette could finish saying the name so dear to her heart, to both their hearts. "Well!," she shouted, "That's my brother! He's your lover, Florangis! You are going to be my sister! He lives for you! He adores you. He is going to show up; & he will marry you." And the tender Fanchette, infused with hope, transported by joy, floating on a sea of delights, barely able to breathe, lifts her beautiful eyes filled with tears of gratitude towards Heaven, presses Rose to her bosom, reaches out with her delicate hand to the young Agathe, & says: "Lussanville! the one & only dear object of my most intense feelings! Ah! God! No! I will not lament my fate any longer: I am going to see my Lussanville again, I am going to be so happy." "My adorable friend," said Agathe, "we are *all* going to be so happy!"

Chapter XLIV

Striking scenes.

"What can be taking them so long!" said the governess to Satinbourg. It's already half an hour. Wait: I think I hear them." She wasn't mistaken.

Lussanville, his governor, & Valincourt, had

gone to see Agathe's mother. The honest fabric merchant didn't believe in revenants; they were standing
in broad daylight: twenty girls, dressed for a wedding,
surrounded her; but she let out a piercing cry, at the
sight of Lussanville's ghost. (More than one girl will
think: "The lovable specter! such a one as this, at
midnight, in my room, would not make me afraid.")
"What is it, Madame! I frighten you?! Get a hold of
yourself; & please tell me... conduct me immediately
to where I might find Mademoiselle Florangis" "Ah,
Monsieur, it's really you!" "People thought you were
dead," said the governor; "That's the reason, my dear
Lussanville, for her fright, which surprises you."
"Ah! be assured of it, Madame: I live, I eat, I drink, I
speak: these are not my *manes* that you see here; it's
me, Lussanville, who is dying with impatience to see
the woman I adore again." "Moderate yourself," said
the old Kathégètes quietly, "&..." "What would you
have me to do? I cannot... I do not know... I feel nothing else... than the desire to see her again, the divine
Fanchette, my love." The fabric merchant recovered
from her initial surprise & fright: but she was feeling
too many emotions at once to be able to respond to
him. In one moment, her mind was filled with
Agathe's happiness, which this event would occasion;
& Fanchette's, whom she loved almost as dearly as
her daughter; & Satinbourg's penchant, which would
cease; & the good Néné's joy; & a thousand other
things. At long last, she was able to explain herself.
"Mademoiselle Fanchette is not here." "Heaven!"
"No, wait! She is with my daughter in a convent,
where neither of them have anything to fear from Financiers, libertines, lotharios, rakehells, & devout old
men. And then she gave him the name & address of
the convent. Lusanville was beside himself. "My
Florangis, my divine bride," he repeated a thousand

times. "Come on, let's go, we've got to hurry." He didn't hear the fabric merchant anymore, who doubtless was going to tell him about her daughter's marriage to Satinbourg & all the rest. He had them take the road to the convent. "One second!" his governor said to him, "Let's pass by the house at least: you need to change clothes & linen; you could frighten everyone dressed like that, & your mistress also, just as you just did Agathe's mother."

"My dear Valincourt," Lussanville said, as they were going along, "don't you marvel that my lover is in the same convent as my sister? Perhaps they already know each other: beautiful women seek each other out; tender souls love to pour their hearts out to one another; What if we were to find them fast friends? Have you made any progress," he asked the old man Kathégètes, "on that project we came up with since my mother passed?" "Yes, my friend, & your sister will soon be free." "What are you saying?" Valincourt interrupted them. "Ah, my dear fellow," took up again Lussanville, "if only you knew the true worth of her heart! An unwitting mistake of the past would not make her friendship less precious to you." And they arrived at Lussanville's house. The two friends went to attend to their toilette; they soon exited again, properly attired & made up; & Cupid himself would have ceded to them at this moment his blindfold, his bow, his arrows, & perhaps his *Psyche*[24]. An elegant cabriolet waits for them; they get in & it departs; & as they passed through the streets of the city of Paris, there wasn't a single old man who saw them that didn't rejoice for them; not a woman whose hearts they didn't tempt; not a young man that didn't

---

[24] *Psyche*: a beautiful girl, in Roman mythology, whom the god Cupid is said to have fallen in love with.

envy them; not a young lady that didn't sigh. While they were flying along to the convent, the old man Kathégètes takes a different route.

The good governor was just leaving the house when one of the Financier's domestics approached him. "This is the tenth time I've come to see you," he said, "& finally I find you; never was anything more pressing." One will learn soon enough what he meant.

Fanchette, Agathe, & Rose were in the bell tower; the two young boarders embraced the tender nun, & exited quickly, without succeeding to inform her what was about to happen; but the Mother Superior thinks that Fanchette was about to be married. And the nanny didn't know what to say, upon seeing her wear the same clothes she had on earlier. "In the end, you want to dress like that, my dear child," she said to her; "Suit yourself; the marriage will still be good." At this moment, Fanchette breaks out in tears; she rushes into the arms of her nanny, & caresses her tenderly; she wants to speak with her, to inform her; Néné wouldn't suffer any delays; she places her ward in Satinbourg's carriage; then jumps into the other carriage. "Let's go," she shouted. And they departed.

Lickety-split they were in the church at the foot of the altar; the minister appears; Satinbourg & the young Agathe rise, Fanchette follows them. "Mercy!" cried Néné, "He's going to marry the both of them!" A short exhortation precedes; the sermon, that two people make one, is pronounced: suddenly, a loud noise is heard, as two young men break through the crowd, pushing people aside with violence: "What are you doing, Ah Heaven!" shouted one of them, "Stop!" He rushes forward & throws himself down before his lover's feet & says to her: "Dear

Fanchette! I was about to lose you!" And feeling no embarrassment at all, while in the presence of an entire crowd of people, he gets up & exhales his passionate soul in a long kiss on her two pink lips. The ceremony stopped. Everyone stared. Then there was a kind of murmuring sound building like the waves of an agitated sea. "What can she lose?" a swarm of young ladies asked themselves, comparing the three charming young men. "If she falls, it won't be too far." Néné rubs her eyes, recognizes Lussanville, rushes up to him & embraces him & the beautiful Florangis together. "And to think it was me who separated you two, my dear children!" she said to them. "I pressured her, I conjured her: she only agreed to it begrudgingly, with crying eyes (that's not the stupidest thing I've done, but God is good & He pardons everything)." "The harm is not as great as you might think, Madame," said Satinbourg, smiling: "Back to your places everyone; we will see this through, to the end." And leaving Fanchette in the arms of her lover, he approaches the minister again with Agathe. "Continue, Monsieur," he said; "all that is nothing more than a misunderstanding." The ceremony ended. Satinbourg's mother & the fashion merchant tried to contain their joyful laughter; & the good Néné understood no more of what had just happened than ancient Romans did of the Sibyls' oracles, than Scandanavians did of the *edda*, than Turks did of the *L'Alcoran*, than our little old politicians do of the affairs of State.

Chapter XLV

What could get out of hand.

A large number of my readers may have forgotten

suddenly that Apatéon had been instructed as to the part the governess had played in Fanchette's first escape, & which he dissimulated knowledge of. Since his return to Paris, he had put feelers out to learn more about her whereabouts & actions. But he could discover no news about his pretty ward, until the morning when Satinbourg was marrying Agathe. That very day, Néné took less precautions that usual; she took no detours, but ran straight to the convent: the devout man's spy discovered Néné's secret; like her, Apatéon's informant thought that the young fabric merchant was about to become Fanchette's husband: he hastened to bring the news to his master.

Little expecting such an event, Apatéon was strangely surprised, & it dissipated his languor. He got himself dressed & flew to the temple, accompanied by his dependents, & followed by his henchmen. He arrives just as everyone is exiting. His presence petrified Néné: Apatéon was petrified by the presence of Valincourt, the sight of Lussanville, & a crowd of very resolute men & women, whom he had stationed around his lover, & who petrified all his cowardly henchmen. But the two young friends & Satinbourg, apparently little disposed to petrification, felt the most violent impulse to act, on seeing the humble, furious, & modest monster. Burning with a desire for vengeance, Valincourt cried out: "Nothing can save you now!" The young Adélaïde's lover was mistaken however: one bad carriage & two good horses saved Apatéon. The hypocrite's henchmen & domestics, on foot unfortunately, couldn't run so fast; they received, in the span of several minutes, as many cane blows with a stick as are administered in one year to all the rogues in the *Fez, Morocco, Algiers, & Tunisia.*

Finally, the dear & tender Lussanville conducts Fanchette to safety. They climb into the carriage with the newlyweds. It was there that this happy young man learned how much he was loved, & that the constancy of his beautiful mistress hadn't wavered for one instant all this time, even when she had believed (mistakenly) in his treachery: he owed all that he knew to the generous Satinbourg, as well as the young Agathe, whose intense friendship for Fanchette had made this virtuous girl's extremely rigorous tests supportable. Florangis, looking ever more lovely in the presence of the man she loved, was never more charming or seductive: Lussanville was drunk on love & pleasure; & the happy Agathe, who thought her friend was going to return to her mother's house to live, burst out with surprise: "My Friend! we are at the convent door!" "Dear lover," said Fanchette to Lussanville, "you owe a visit, that I am making you pay, to the tender Adélaïde, your sister, & my friend, who just this morning announced to me for the first time your return & my happiness." "My sister!... you know her! you love each other! Divine Florangis! Ah! that's exactly what I was hoping so desirously should happen, when I learned you were both residing at the same convent." And they entered, & Sister Rose appeared, & all that could be heard were cries of surprise & joy. "Where," asked Lussanville, "is Valincourt? How come I don't see him?" At the mention of his name, so dear & so sad to the ears of the tender nun, she let out a deep sigh: then she pronounced with a faltering voice: "He lives!" & she faints. "Alas!" said Fanchette, "how miserable it is to love when one is separated by eternal obstacles!" While his sister was being revived, Lussanville responded: "Maybe we know how to make them stop."

Everyone had followed the young newlyweds

& Fanchette: they were encouraged to continue on & make their way to the place of celebration. Rose returned to her room in the convent; the tender Florangis, on leaving her, promised that she would return in a few hours; & they separated.

No sooner had they begun to loosen up & enjoy themselves at such pastimes as their betters don't participate in but leave for the people to enjoy, because they themselves would turn red in the face if they had to act happy in this way, because these proud dominators of the human race have altogether other kinds of amusement, which are: to corrupt the mothers of families, seduce girls, & precipitate them into debauchery; when *they* enter into most holy matrimony, the most tender of commitments, they do so with a sad & dreary air; they would abolish solemnities, in order to escape, as far as possible, all duty & responsibility, – that's their mores for you! O people! you would be lost if such mores were passed down to you! Dance then, & be merry at your wedding parties & celebrations; that your girls might learn that it is at these festivals only that a young man might be allowed to squeeze their delicate hands... scorn them, both the atrabilious, sneaky, hypocritical, intolerant, jealous, & devout men, as well as the contemptuous & contemptible libertines & lotharios. Act like *people*, a word that – o sacred name – SAINT LOUIS, most beloved of kings, never pronounced without a visible demonstration of feeling... But where was I?[25] I was saying that no sooner had they begun to divert themselves than Agathe, Satinbourg, Fachette, & Lussanville got up from the table, & the bride went to dance a minuet, when one of those government officials,

---

[25] Original footnote: This chapter is one of the ones conserved intact, & which the old man Kathégètes confirms.

who is charged with ensuring the public order amongst citizens, was seen to enter by the door. Everyone grows agitated: the boisterous wedding guests run to fetch their swords, while the mothers, wives, sisters, & their mistresses hold them back: the groom, Lussanville, & Valincourt rise to receive this officer, showing him consideration & respect.

Chapter XLVI

Wherein a hypocrite avenges himself.

"Fear not that we might be lacking in any way towards you, Monsieur," said Lussanville. "Tell your guards to be at their ease: we respect you, & not just the magistrature you represent, whence you derive your power, but also our sovereign himself, in whom we recognize both the source & plenitude of all that we possess: speak; we will confidently give an account of our conduct to the minsters of the law."

"You are, gentlemen," responded this *terrifying* man, "such as those I hoped to find. The magistrature, at the instance of a certain Monsieur Apatéon, issued to the latter, sometime ago, an order for the arrest of a young man, whom he accused of meditating *adulteries & seductions* amongst honest people, whom he says he is a friend of. He added that, only seeking the best for this young man, he would hold him in custody until he had informed his parents, & gotten their instructions. Lastly, he solicited that his ward be returned to him, whom bad counsels, he insinuated, had alienated from him. The manner in which all that was executed appeared to warrant some attention. Today it is a much more serious complaint:

it is quite unusual: these ladies, & you, gentlemen, should be interested to hear it.

To Your Eminence, &c.,

Philotès Philogunes Théophile Benigne Job Bonaventure Théodore Dieudonné Clément Simplicien Boniface Nicaise Bon Gilles Blaise Nabuchdonosor Apatéon, a bourgeois of Paris, former churchwarden of his parish, of the brotherhoods of... &c., &c., very humbly entreats you.

KNOW THIS: that the aforementioned having been provisioned with your orders to return to the right path a girl, a poor orphan, whose care had been entrusted to him by the father of the same, before having rendered account before his eminence the Judge, he would have effectively & newly encountered this small setback: That he would have conducted her even to a solitary place, several leagues distant from the Capital, in order to sever all ties, by this salutary retreat, to the bad habits & frequentations of the aforesaid orphan: That he would have been for the duration of several days together with her: That by pure kindness, & desire to win her over to God, he would have suffered one of his companions, too young to be dangerous, to accompany her: That despite this indulgence, & other acts of kindness, capable of touching the most hardened of hearts, this little, impudent person having apparently found the means to make her situation & whereabouts known to young libertines *whom perhaps she had favored (something that Christian charity alone seeks to prevent from happening), he would see himself suddenly attacked in the middle of the night, by a group of armed men who, not content with breaking down gates & doors, pillaging his house, removing the aforesaid poor orphan girl & her young companion, would have also so grievously & so feloniously maltreated, him, the above-mentioned Philotès Philogunes, &c. Apatéon, who would have been still in bed at that time: That by an instance of darkest perfidy & monstrous ingratitude, he would have heard the aforementioned poor orphan, at the time of her abduction, excite her ravishers to take away with them also, him, Apatéon; which he suspected to have been said with the intent of exposing him to cruel punishments, & perhaps to murder him, if he had not been protected by the holy maxim, that prescribes believing in the good, & never in evil: That happily for him, being an infirm old man, a man respected in his neighborhood, & qualified as above, he had been found, by chance, when the Monsieur Count d'A*** passed by his house; the which latter gentleman having heard the horrible tumult in progress, would have entered, with the express purpose of providing aid; but that this Lord, finding himself insufficiently strong to resist a band of wicked men, should resort only to obtaining by his remonstrances that the supplicant be left behind: That he would have learned that at a certain distance, the said sire Count d'A*** having rejoined his men, who* *had gone on before him, had undertaken to give said abductors chase: That one of them, whom he knew not, had profited by the disorder that the attack caused, to make off with the aforementioned poor orphan & her companion: that the same Count d'A***, having gotten hold of several of her abductors, would have conducted them to a house belonging to the Marquis de C***, with the purpose of drawing from them necessary information as to their infamy, as well as the names of their accomplices: That those who had employed these men, having learned of their detention, would have surprised him by an order to deliver them, & that by this means the supplicant would have seen himself deprived of the information he expected: That the supplicant despaired of learning any more information about his ward, when on the morning of this day, God, who does not permit that crime triumphs, had wanted him to learn that the aforementioned poor orphan was contracting a clandestine marriage, with a* quidam, *perfectly unknown to the said Philotès Philogunes, &c. Apatéon: That being charged by the father of the aforementioned poor orphan, to provide for her, & wanting to do so, for the love of God, as also in memory of his deceased friend, despite the frequent escapades (if this term suffices) of the aforementioned poor orphan, he would be, in his condition of feebleness & illness, compelled to form legal opposition to this celebration, the which would have been found concluded: That his presence having frightened the aforementioned poor* *orphan, she would have probably excited three* quidams *to insult him & menace him, with such excessiveness, that he, supplicant, former churchwarden, &c. would have been constrained to seek safety in prompt flight.*

For all said facts the supplicant offers proof & conviction; requires right & justice from you, your Grace; asks provisorily that the aforementioned poor orphan, as having contracted marriage illegally, & clandestinely, in respect to her tutor, should be returned unto salutary retreats that are appropriate for those who must weep their entire life for having forfeited their virtue. And wishing you well, I am

– Philotès Philogunes, &c. Apatéon.

To such hypocrisy, perfidy, & calumny, a mixture of horror & indignation was displayed on all faces present. "Far be it from me to wish to bother you during your celebrations," continued the justice officer. "Tell me only your principal means of defense; I will present them to the magistrate, who has already made some inquiries, & before whom it will be enough for you to present yourselves tomorrow. Enough said."

It was then that, despite the kind Fanchette's wishes, Lussanville & Valincourt, – generous enough to have formed a plan never to invoke the protection of the laws against the attempts made by the Marquis de C***, the Count d'A***, or the unworthy Apatéon, – gave a complete account of all the indignities these latter three men had been guilty of. The officer smiled as he took down their depositions.

When they had finished, the good Néné also wanted to dictate something in turn; but she asked that the account be kept secret. She was right; her pact with the Count d'A***, although extorted, is a dark stain on her story, which she will always be ashamed of. The officer expressed much astonishment, when he learned that the beautiful Florangis was not the person who had just become united with Satinbourg, & that it was Monsieur Lussanville whom she was going to marry: he added this detail & left quite satisfied.

Everyone proceeded to enjoy themselves. And Fanchette, accompanied by her dear Lussanville, the newlyweds, & Valincourt himself whom was brought along, returned to the convent, where the tender Rose must have been impatiently waiting for her friend.

Chapter XLVII

What will elicit pleasure.

All that pleasant youth was waiting in the parlor when Sister Rose appeared. Valincourt stood behind the others. "Dear friend, lift the veil," said the young Agathe: my husband & Monsieur," she added, pointing out Valincourt, "are like tender brothers to you, like Monsieur de Lussanville." And Sister Rose, who was referred to as Adélaïde anymore, does as she was told. The first thing her eyes alight on is her lover. Her eyes well up with tears: she grows pale; & feeling her knees buckling underneath her, she sits down. Valincourt's heart was torn in two: he approaches her: but the two forbidden lovers, held back for the strongest reasons, do not dare to exchange a single word: they don't ask each other questions nor respond except by sighing. Lussanville looked at them; he pressed Fanchette's hands in his own & spoke to her in a low voice, when the old man Kathégètes arrived.

"I have strange news to report," he said taking his ward aside: "Your uncle the Financier, while returning home yesterday after a night out drinking, half a league outside the city, was attacked by a man whose wife he had just debauched: he received two mortal wounds; he was brought back to his house covered in blood. By dint of effort, he regained consciousness for several moments. As he believed you were dead, he gave all his fortune to your sister; adding to his will *that he was in good conscience certain that the vows of his niece had been forced on her; that his sister, on her deathbed, had shown signs of remorse for having constrained her; & that she would have desired to live if only to repair the wrong she had done: he entreated the ecclesiastical & secular judges to honor the wishes of a dying man, who only wanted to tell the truth.* He lasted only a few more minutes after this declaration. I was informed of it this morning, one minute after I had quit you. As the business of the cassation of your sister's vows were going to be adjudicated in the morning, I ran to her defense attorney, to whom I communicated the testament. Nothing could have been more apropos: your feelings for your sister; your disinterestedness, that the lawyer demonstrated, together with this testimony of your uncle, excited the admiration of your judges, & softened them: your sister is a free woman: read for yourself, here's the pronouncement that was just given to me."

Lussanville, although affected by the sad news of his uncle, could not contain his joy knowing that his sister's bonds had been broken; & when he was sure that nobody in the convent would be able to hear him, he held this conversation with Adélaïde: "Dear Sister, you know what my feelings for you have always been: it was with heartfelt regret that I saw you make the sacrifice of your freedom, to enchain yourself by oaths that your heart didn't second. But, what could I do? Heaven has deprived us of our mother: I must cherish her memory; she loved me... too much, maybe, & acted towards you like a wicked stepmother. You will remember that the day after your fateful day, I pretended to have need of your signature: I asked you to sign your name to several blank sheets of paper. Equipped with these necessary instruments, my governor & I have acted in your name, with great success & under great secrecy, such that we have had your vows annulled by authentic court order, without anyone in this house knowing about it yet." "Heaven! what joy!" cried out Fanchette, Agathe, & Satinbourg all at the same time. Lussanville continued: "In these affairs, I could only act on your behalf; & I acted only the part of a witness in your favor: your signed sheets of blank paper have become, in my & M. Kathégètes' hands, complaints, requests to the high-ranking Church officials, sovereign courts: I had even, before I was detained by the Marquis de C***, been able to touch our prelate's heart & win him over to our side. Everything we put our hands to succeeded. Our uncle, whom a tragic accident has just taken from us, has contributed, on his last breath, to your freedom; he disclosed the feelings of our mother, her remorses, acknowledgement of the constraint she used on you; by the same act, he wills everything he possessed to you. I dare glimpse a happy outcome for you in the near future. This charming girl here who consents willingly to my felicity will join you again for a short while: everything is in preparation for our sacred union; & on the day I plan to marry my lover, we will sign the judgment: you will exit, the two of you, at the same time; we will be inseparable."

It wasn't long before everyone was offering their sincere felicitations to the tender Adélaïde, who sought to read her destiny in Valincourt's eyes. The unfortunate young man was in a sorry state, which he could not get over still. It was getting late; everyone departed. Fanchette, bathed in Agathe's tears, returned to her room at the convent. Lussanville had a hard time leaving, followed by his governor & Valincourt. The newlyweds, borne on wings of desire, flew to the temple of love, desire, & hymen; & the good Néné was careful not to return to Apatéon's house.

Chapter XLVIII

Wherein atrocities redound upon their authors.

De Lussanville & all his friends rose early the next morning, Satinbourg included. The young Agathe's happy spouse, whom Love had just surfeited with its delicious favors, understood nothing of Valincourt's coldness. "You are surprised," his pretty companion said to him; "but you don't know everything. Apatéon..." "How's that!" "Yes." "Is that even possible, good God!" "Unfortunately, yes." If my reader does not understand, it's because this conversation was not the clearest one: but it's like that with newlyweds; they are laconic: they know what they are talking about: they believe everyone else understands their half words too. "Alas!" replied the young fabric merchant, "How sorry I feel for them! However, that would not stop me."

Soon they all got together again: they had to present themselves before the magistrate; they rush to Fanchette's convent. They find her made up with the help of her dear Adélaïde. She was never so fetching. Her beautiful hair, which had received the most graceful contours as a result of a *complimentary* curling, was unadulterated by any auburn powder: they saw her hair such as it was, decorated with flowers, embellished with ivory & diamonds, brushed into long tresses, that covered her chignon. Over a corset that pinched her exceptionally small waist, she wore a dress whose tissue, silver & silk, blinded one's sight, elegantly garnished, becoming to her, & made by the best tailor in town: on her pretty foot she wore a slipper of pearls, fastened by a brilliant, oblong buckle made of love knots, of exquisite taste.[26]

And where did Fanchette acquire all this finery? Lussanville, before his trip to Bayonne, had ordered it, in concert with Néné: on his return, all of it was found to be ready, & from the moment he was free, he had these beautiful things carried to the convent where Fanchette was staying. And why was she dressing up in them! Dear, curious reader, the memoirs I draw from say nothing as to her motives: but, if you like, I will act as other historians, my confreres, do: I will make things up, & I will tell you this: as all women, even the most honest & wise among them, being a little coquettish, Fanchette didn't wish to appear before the magistrate without all her advantages on display. *Or*, indignant at the Marquis de C*** & the Count d'A***, who had never had legitimate views, she wanted to show them what they could

---

[26] Original footnote: They were what Monsieur Apatéon had imagined.

have had if they had chosen the way of virtue & honor; *Or*, she dressed like this make Monsieur Apatéon die of rage; *Or*, she wanted everyone to envy the lot of a lover she adored. *Or*... Dear reader, imagine her motives for yourself, I give you free rein; they will be as little founded as my own.

One could not grow tired of admiring the beautiful Florangis: Agathe, with most lively transports, with a prettier, subtler, & more tender attitude than the day before, gave her a thousand kisses; Lussanville quivered; & the good Néné muttered between her teeth: "I would stab myself now, if the Count...." They departed. On the way, Satinbourg said to Valincourt: "No, I would not hesitate: you are sure to be loved; the fault was involuntary: must the audacity of a villain make two young lovers unhappy who are made for each other? I will go even further & say this: If the beautiful Adélaïde had forgotten herself & was seduced by a momentary pleasure, or even got carried away by... that would have constituted consent: but when she repented it immediately afterwards, & she gave her heart to you, it would have been hard & cruel not to be touched. You are in quite a different situation; she is innocent; you cannot doubt it." Valincourt, without responding, lowered his eyes. My readers will soon learn the denouement of his adventure. And we have arrived.

Lussanville & the beautiful Florangis entered first, Agathe & Satinbourg followed them; as did the governess & the good Néné; the fashion merchant, with a dozen of her girls; Valincourt, agitated, sullen, his eyes glued to the ground, & red in the face, pulled up the rear. The magistrate received them with that genuine affability that is normal for him. He had in hand the writ from the day before, which he had just finished reading. He asked new questions of each one of those present, with the exception of the beautiful Florangis, to whom he only addressed flattering compliments, without mentioning a word of the business at hand. In spite of himself, his eyes looked for that charming foot of hers, which its conquests had made famous: he smiled. Finally, he gave this speech:

"Your adversaries are going to appear soon: know that under the wise government that rules over us, it is impossible for crime to be hidden for long. I had been well informed, before even Monsieur Apatéon presented his last request; & I have been provided with an exact account of all his steps, since the first request that he had brought forward made me conceive some suspicions... You," he said to Néné, "show me the document that Mademoiselle Florangis' father gave to you." And the nanny presents it to him. "This authoritative act," he continued, "& all that you have done: I praise your efforts. And you," he said to the old Kathégètes, "whence comes it that you didn't address yourself to me, from the first moment that your pupil vanished? The magistrates are the fathers, & the born defenders, of all those who are oppressed. You, Monsieur de Lussanville, you have acted imprudently at times, which would be punishable if your adversaries had not always been the aggressors; or if even you had been too grievously outraged to be able to moderate your steps: from now on, avoid evil men; the purest virtue will be stained by them, & one must rather flee them than combat them. As for Monsieur Valincourt, his affair is messy: he will need to provide me with more ample explanations in the presence of his adversary." The magistrate spoke of Dolsans to the fashion merchant; one could see he knew about everything. Finally, he came to Fanchette; he approved her behavior in everything: "You will be, Mademoiselle," he said to her, "a model for your sex, & every parent must pray to Heaven to have girls like you."

He had just finished speaking when the Count d'A***, the Marquis de C***, & the *modest* Apatéon are announced. Their surprise was not small when they noticed, on entering, the numerous assembly that awaited them. Apatéon saw, above all, in each of the girls whom the fashion merchant had brought with her, witnesses to the violence he had made against the young Agathe. The magistrate spoke for some time with the three guilty parties in particular; they were seen to turn red in the face & grow pale, each in his turn. But nothing equaled the comical groveling figure that Apatéon cut, when he realized that all his wickedness had been uncovered & was ready to be exposed to the light of day: he was clasping his hands; his body leaned forward; his face was distraught; he let out several painful sighs; he lifted his eyes towards Heaven with an expression of rage & despair; he brought them back down & laid them sadly on Fanchette; he held back his tears; he responded by bowing with his body towards the ground as benignly as possible: but all his grimaces & gestures were useless: he had been unmasked.

Fanchette heard, with as much satisfaction as surprise, as the magistrate ordered the Marquis de C*** to give back to Lussanville the portrait & the other presents he had taken. Those things, imprudently shown to the Asiatic man, served to open the magistrate's eyes: he let the young Florangis hear about it; but without entering into any great detail. Fanchette's eyes grew increasingly wider with surprise when she saw the two proud abductors kneeling before her, begging her to choose one of them for a husband, & to receive his hand & loyalty. They could not look on her again, on her bewitching foot & all her attractions, which her attire & toilette gave a particular shine to, & which blinded them, – without new fires of lust kindling in their loins. "A poor orphan," the young person responded to them, "does not keep such high views of herself, Messieurs." And holding her hand out to Lussanville, she said, "Here is the man who chose me first, whom I prefer to any other man in the universe: he loves me, I am sure of it; he esteems me, respects me, & above all, is virtuous."

And the poor Philotès-Philogunes Apatéon wept profusely. "What do you want from them, Mademoiselle?" asked the judicious magistrate. "I want them to forget me, Monsieur," responded Florangis: "I forgive them: would that they might change; let them choose among their equals a good companion for themselves, & live happily ever after with her! As for Monsieur Apatéon, I will always remember him as a friend of my father's, who had shown kindness to me. Where is the man who can say, at the end of a long career, that his virtue had never once been belied! I am happy now, would that he could be too!" The magistrate expressed high praise for such generous sentiments, & after having gotten additional information as concerned Valincourt, he dismissed the beautiful Florangis, Lussanville, & their friends.

Chapter XLIX

Fanchette recovers her celestial-blue slipper.

One remembers doubtless that the Asiatic man had

been a witness to Lussanville's deliverance. He had only just understood that the marquis & the count, proud of their position & birth, substituted pleasure for duty; substituted their unbridled passion for justice & honesty; & as soon as he had learned this, he decided to break all ties with them: he sold the little house that his nascent friendship had caused him to purchase, embellish, & occupy in the vicinity of Monsieur de C***, – & he returned to Paris.

Ever searching for Fanchette, whom he could not find; sure however that Lussanville was free, he wished to put a damper on his hopeless love. Such was his disposition of mind, when he received on that very same day, from Pondicherry, the news he had been impatiently waiting for, that the governor of that city, by whom he had previously been unjustly accused of having bought & sold illicit goods, & of having passed dangerous intelligence to the Commander of Madras, had recognized his innocence, written letters to the court to reverse the accusations that had been brought against him, re-established his name & honor in the colony, & permitted the embarkment of all his riches; from the Orient, a communication that three of his vessels, richly loaded, had just arrived in port; from the public prosecutor in Paris, that all the affairs he had left behind him, on his departure, were finally accommodated, the seizures lifted, the decrees purged, & that a security payment for the entire amount could not dare be requested, – all which made him a friend to his creditors again. So much good news would have been even sweeter if he had had with him, to share it with, his son, his unfortunate family, or that pretty Florangis girl, whom he still believed was the niece of the fashion merchant; but he didn't forget to rejoice with his son's good instructor.

The reasons that had made him have his death published three years earlier, keep his return to Paris a secret from his former acquaintances, & change his name – were no longer necessary: he came forward to present himself to those who were formerly his friends & associates. His first visit was to Monsieur Delaunage, that old neighbor of Fanchette's father, who wanted to make her his mistress & to marry her; who gave her presents that she returned; who had just sold his interest in the fabric business to Satinbourg. The old merchant's surprise was extreme; at first, he didn't want to believe his eyes nor his friend. Finally, convinced that he was looking at Monsieur Rosin, he embraced him tenderly, asked him about his wife, his son... "She is dead," Rosin interrupted him, "& my son is lost." "Lost!" "Yes, lost, somewhere in Paris, where I had sent him. Alas! all my investigations & those of his governor have until now been fruitless." "But one does not just get lost: you will find him. By the good order that reigns in this capital, the best-kept secrets are always discovered, sooner or later." "You give me a little hope." "Your niece must have been overjoyed to see you?" "My niece! eh! do you have any news about her whereabouts?" "You haven't seen her yet!" "I don't know where to find her." "Ah!, what pleasure you will both have! she's a marvel, your niece: a girl... If only the young Satinbourg were here now: he never stops singing her praises: tomorrow..." "If you don't mind, I'd like to see her today." "Like you, I don't know where to find her either: there's some talk of a convent... Satinbourg knows all about it; he can tell you; but we cannot see him until tomorrow. By the way, your niece will look like the spitting image of your sister, when in her youth, her graces, her resplendent beauty made all hearts bend a knee to her." "You put off the moment of my seeing her, & then you augment the desire I have. She is, you say, beautiful like her mother?" "I believe she exceeds her in beauty." And Rosin trembled. He thought to himself: "My niece sounds like she resembles the beautiful Fanchette... she has all my sister's traits: she will stand in for my son, for my mistress... & because in life there is a power that legitimizes the feelings she inspires in me, I am rich: I will profit thereby." "Tomorrow, then, Monsieur Delaunage?" he said. "Yes, tomorrow we'll go together & pay Satinbourg a visit; a new wife, I still remember it well, makes one sleep in late; we will surprise him in bed; you will get to know..." "This Satinbourg fellow is married?" "He just got married to your niece's friend." "Ah! that comforts me." "Honestly, he only did it to please her..." An unexpected visitor showed up: & Rosin, transported by joy, departed.

On the following day, before morning had broken, Rosin woke up, got dressed, held in his hands the pretty celestial-blue slipper that he had lifted off Fanchette's foot, & hurries off to Delaunage's house. The old man was surprised to see him so early. "Do you want to interrupt," he said to him laughing, "two newlyweds after they have only just now begun to enjoy a beneficial sleep, as they restore their exhausted strength? It's too early. Wait awhile." "What do you expect?" responded Rosin; "I'm burning with impatience: I've lost everything that was dear to me in life; a son, my only hope; a beautiful mistress, wise in the midst of abductions; a true phoenix in a word; so seductive... this pretty shoe adorned her." "Your pheonix," said Delaunage coldly, "cannot hold a candle to Mademoiselle Florangis in that department.

You will see."

       The two friends spoke for some time about their affairs, about Rosin's fortune, & his adventures. "You didn't share any news of yourself to that poor Florangis?" asked Delaunage. "I wrote many times;" he responded, "but I never received a response: it was only later that I learned of their deaths. Only recently, I heard that among the various vessels that carried my letters, the first one sank, & the others were seized by the English." "It appears to me that in those distant climates, Fortune grew tired of always working against you." "As you know, I left Paris with the little that remained of my first fortune: it was a crime in the eyes of my correspondents: I was accused of bad faith; some tried to ruin my reputation: legal proceedings were filed against me; & all the weight of their hatred pressed down hard on me: I foresaw it & expected it. Florangis (my sister's husband) was virtuous, but pusillanimous; my sister was too affected; I would have given an arm & a leg to spare them the ills they had suffered. I invested my funds advantageously, & I was employed as a scribe on the vessel that transported me. On arriving in Pondicherry, I was in possession of the books of a famous trader, & at the same time I had the freedom to traffic on my own account. Everything I did succeeded: I gained the good will of my principal benefactor, as a result of the good order I had kept his affairs in: my own affairs flourished: at the end of several years, we became partners. Everything went from good to better; because I became more daring, & luck continued to watch over me, our fortune doubled in no time. My associate died: the English took Pondicherry: I had rendered important services, before the declaration of war, to divers traders of that nation; they manifested their gratitude to me, amidst general public distress, by assuring me of the possession of my wealth: I was the only person, for the moment, who hadn't suffered by the takeover. But this favor was the cause of my subsequent loss. As soon as peace was established between the two nations, those who envied what my good fortune had secured for me, didn't fail to blacken my reputation in the eyes of the new governor. With each passing day, the thunder clouds grew larger over my head: the danger I was in became pressing; I thought to get away with my life & a small portion of my possessions; & fearing that my son, whom I had sent to Paris, might be arrested, I renewed my wishes to his instructor not to make an appearance before our connections & acquaintances in Paris. My enemies' hatred had poisoned their minds to the degree that, in order to escape entirely, I had my death publicly announced; everyone believed it, even my son; only his guide knew the truth. Valincourt (that's the name I made him assume) was in love when he heard the news: he disappeared not long thereafter, & the object of his feelings had no idea even what had happened to him. The person I had hired to escort him to Paris, rejoined me, informed me of this deplorable news: I was desperate. We came back, the two of us, to France, with what little I could take with me of my riches. Today, everything has changed; I've been cleared of all wrongdoing in Pondicherry; & if I should find my dear Valincourt, as well as my niece, I would have everything I desire in life."

When Rosin finished speaking, it was time to go visit Satinbourg at his home; he departs with Delaunage. But the young couple had already left the house by the time they got there: Fanchette's convent is mentioned, that they were going there. The two friends hurry to the convent. The pleasant Adélaïde alone receives them & informs them that Satinbourg & his young companion hadn't stopped by. Delaunage asks for Fanchette. The young nun thought she should protect her. Rosin is vividly struck by the charming sister's graces; his heart, easy to be inflamed, grows interested in her: he speaks with her for several moments, says some sweet things to her. Adélaïde considered him closely: some traits, a voice she thought she recognized, caught her attention. "How did one resolve, Madame, to bury such charms in a cloister?" "Buried! Me! I'd be in despair." "You are not..." "Yes." "And..." "In two days. You know Monsieur Satinbourg; in two days you will know everything." "Ah Heaven! Madame, I was in love with a very beautiful young person, whom I saw twice. I fell head over heels in love with her from the first moment; but you are her equal, I swear it. This slipper was hers." "Let me see it. But, I think..." "May I have it back again?" "Come again tomorrow & I'll give it back to you." Rosin was delighted that this little gem gave him the pretext to see the pretty cloistered person again: he consents & departs with the old merchant.

Adélaïde, on seeing the cute little slipper, knew that it belonged to no one else than Fanchette. But how in the world did it get into the hands of a man known by Satinbourg? She runs to her friend, whom she calls her tender sister: she catches her up on what just happened, & presents to her the slipper. Fanchette recognizes it with surprise; she recounts how, & under what circumstances, she lost it; she looks for its match, finds it, & puts them both on. Two hours later they are still talking about the same subject; & the young Agathe appears.

Chapter L

New abduction.

"My dear Florangis, here is some more troubling news: an uncle, whom I have never heard of, drops in out of nowhere & comes to torment us." "What are you talking about, dear Agathe!" "Yes, your uncle, a Monsieur Rosin; Monsieur Delaunage & he, who just left us, came to tell us the news." "Heavens! What an unexpected delight!" "You're delighted! but you still don't know..." "Ah! if only I could see him." "Be careful! When you learn of his plans, & his arrival, which ought to have caused us all the greatest joy, you will find that they bring us only sadness. Your uncle burns with desire to see you again: he has complete power over you: he will never consent to your union with Monsieur Lussanville." "Ah! God!" "No, there's more: he lost his wife, & his only son; he has brought back with him his immense riches; he wants to make you the mistress of all his fortune by marrying you. Those are his plans." "My feelings & my tears will change his thinking." "Don't flatter yourself: he has seen you, we don't know how; & he loves you before knowing you even. There is only one way for you to free yourself from a thousand hassles in one shot; Monsieur Lussanville knows nothing about this; let's go inform him; we will stay at his place all day; this evening you will marry him; then, tomorrow we will go see your uncle who, not having yet registered his return to Paris with the authorities, will have no say over the matter." Fanchette, troubled, hesitated: Adélaïde backed up the good Agathe, to decide the matter.

The two friends exited the convent in order to visit the fashion merchant, where they could alert

Lussanville & the good Néné: at the convent portal, a man was holding a conversation with a young girl, who mentioned Valincourt's name; Fanchette & Satinbourg's wife stopped dead in their tracks, stared at the young person: she looked like one of those miserable women who willingly forfeit their citizenship for certain emoluments, & who belong to a shameful class apart, an impure exhalation of corruption found in large cities: Agathe & Fanchette turned their gaze away because they felt ashamed for her. This girl was the little Lolote, who had just recognized Rosin. At that moment, Valincourt's father's eyes crossed those of the beautiful Florangis'. "Yes! it's her," he blurts out, "She has... look, that pretty little slipper on that I had just given to the lovely nun. I haven't yet had a chance to examine her features close up; but what an effect they have on me! If that was... I cannot let this opportunity slip out of my hands again." These last words strike Fanchette's ear: she remembers the stranger who wanted to save her one day; she hurries to climb into the standing carriage that Agathe had brought with her & which was waiting for her; they close the doors, & in this way she leaves herself to her destiny. The coach driver, whom Rosin had taken the time to speak a word with moments earlier, followed the orders he had given him.

The carriage stops after a short distance, the door opens, & Rosin appears, offering his hand to Fanchette, who, on seeing herself in front of the stranger's house, lets out a cry, & clasps onto Agathe.

Chapter LI

An unexpected obstacle.

"Pardon me, Mademoiselle," said Rosin, "for a small deception, which only the impatience of meeting you suggested. Don't be so alarmed, which is insulting to me, ladies: there is nobody who honors virtue united with beauty more than I do." Fanchette felt reassured by this discourse: the stranger took her hand; she didn't retract it: it seemed to her that in her heart this stranger should hold a place beside Lussanville: she was the first to pressure Agathe to give into the suggestions he made to them to enter his house: the young wife of Satinbourg could not get over her surprise; but Valincourt's name, which they had heard dropped to the stranger by Lolote earlier, excited her curiosity; she gave in.

"If what my heart tells me is true," Rosin said to her emotionally, "you are the person I despaired of ever finding again. Fate deprived me of a cherished sister." "A sister!" interrupted Fanchette. "And that sister is that?" she continued. "I see her traits in you. Her name was Florangis, I am Rosin." "You! my uncle, it's you! It's him, dear Agathe!" Fanchette always carried with her the box that contained her mother's portrait, & the letter that, on her death bed, she had written to her brother. "Here," she said to Rosin, "is the portrait of my mother." "As soon as he saw it, his eyes welled up with tears" "O my daughter!" he cried out, "pressing her to his chest, it's only now that fate stops persecuting me: it took my son from me, but it answers my wishes by the only object that could console me for so great a loss." "I've found my father again, dear Agathe. I will adore you: you will have a son in Lussanville: together we..." "Ah!

my daughter! What is this paper?" "It's for you. I always respected the prohibition of opening it, which as you can see is written in my father's hand." Rosin kisses the letter from his sister, breaks the seal, & then reads it:

Somewhere in the world where you breathe, dear Rosin, indifferent or still caring, there is elsewhere a heart that still loves you, that desires your presence, that thinks shiveringly on that very moment when, frightening as it might seem, the same mother who gave birth to me gave birth to you. How many times has the difference in our names made others mistake us for lovers! O happy times! O my brother! the same blood that flows through your veins flows through mine; but it circulates now more slowly in me. A cruel enemy, the spouse, or rather the shrew of that lover whom I admitted to you my weakness for, hasn't thought herself revenged enough by the unhappiness she caused us; she adds injury to insult, & poison to that... she's the guilty one, I have no doubt about it: in several hours, I will be dead: my daughter loses a mother, instructed by experience. Oh! why aren't you here with me! you would receive my last breath; you would console me, you would sustain my miserable husband; you would take in my daughter, you would replace me with Fanchette... Fanchette! My dear brother, my friend, do you understand the horror inherent in the poor Fanchette's situation? I shudder to think about it, she is so beautiful & innocent; she whom I leave, as I was left, at the center of a corrupt & seductive world, & she will lose her father any day now, whose staggering health grows weaker each day. In the name of God, of rights of blood, of our tender & constant friendship, dear Rosin, if you return some day, take her into your arms, my daughter, as if she were your own; if you can, make her happy; protect her at least, defend her from her mother's murderers, keep her from going astray... Rosin! you know me; I am out of my mind; my friend, if my daughter should go astray, it would be my fault: in this case even, forgive her, lead her back from the edge: neither vice, nor crime, should make us be hated by our parents or our friends: that's the craven pretext of hard hearts, to focus on flaws while neglecting the virtues they should love. Brother, I encourage you to think of my daughter's happiness: I beg you to ensure it by all possible means. I order you; the state of exhaustion that I find myself in gives me the right: remember that that immortal soul, that was fond of you, that the poison will not touch, will have its eyes focused on Fanchette & on you. It will read in your heart from on high the most secret thoughts. My pain begins to cease: a supernatural light seems to shine on me. My strength is gone... Rosin! Fanchette, my daughter: my brother, treat her as if she were yours, &....

It was impossible to read the half-formed, scribbled characters that followed. Fanchette & her uncle shed tears. What thoughts agitated them! Rosin said to her:

"So! it's you, daughter! you! this Lussan-ville's lover, whose mother... You! who ought to detest everything that is connected with that abominable mother of his! And I thought I was being unjust, the day I saw him save you from danger, when I felt that I hated him. However, my daughter, your happiness is all that I care for: my sister orders it; at the expense of my heart, more yours then you think, I will do it." Fanchette, distraught, unmoving, sighed & kept silent for several moments. Then lifting her eyes timidly to look at her uncle: "If only you knew him!" she said: "Ah! if only you knew him!" "All his virtues," he responded, "if he has any, mean nothing any longer: my daughter, this note that you yourself have just given to me ought to dash them all to pieces in your eyes & separate you both forever." "Ah! God! I'd rather be dead!... Is Lussanville a criminal then, for having been born of a criminal mother! He has so many virtues! Dear Agathe, write to my Nanny: ask her to come; her testimony will be less suspect than my own." "Am I hearing this right? the son of the woman who deprived you of a mother is so dear to you! an odious blood..." "Stop! Ah! uncle! my father! I love him; but he is so worthy of it! & his sister...; the one by friendship, the other by love, have so much control over my heart; must I break them then, such pleasant ties?!" "Your mother is dead! What perils, what unhappiness, did she who deprived you of her... what hasn't she caused! Unfortunate girl!" "I forgive her of them, my cruelest enemy: & my lover... We were hoping to enjoy such pure felicity! His sister, whom you met, whose religious vows are dissolved." "That lovely girl I spoke with?" "One & the same. His sister & the young Valincourt." "The young Valincourt!"

"Did I say something wrong: you look upset! his name was mentioned to you when we left the convent: do you happen to know him? a young man," Fanchette continued animatedly, "who for three years now was believed to be lost, the son of a rich trader from Pondicherry, the friend of my lover, who..." "He's my son then! & it's you who are telling me this! O my dear Fanchette! Where can I find him?"

Rosin had barely finished speaking when Lussanville, Valincourt, & Agathe's husband showed up.

"Ah! cousin," Fanchette cried out, approaching Valincourt & standing in front of him! "Your father: my uncle." The young man's governor entered: he notices his pupil & runs to him; he lifts him up & carries him in his arms to his father. How sweet a moment this was! "O God! what a happy day this is," said Rosin, "that reunites me with all who are most dear to me in life! My son! my dear son! who is it then who separated you from the friend I had watching over you?"

The young Valincourt was going to answer his father; to tell him of Apatéon's wickedness, of his friendship for Lussanville, & perhaps of Adélaïde: when a messenger from the magistrate appeared & invited Rosin to follow him. Rosin cast a jealous glance at Lussanville, begged Fanchette to make herself at home, & left in the company of his son.

Whilst they were leaving, Fanchette asked Lussanville why her nanny hadn't joined them. "I'm not sure," responded the kind young man: "But she's the one who made me deliver Agathe's note." And the tender Florangis was not at all reassured: she absolutely had to see her, & begged them go find her.

Chapter LII

Bibi.

Rosin received from the magistrate new proof that his troubles were over; assurances of protection from the monarch to continue his trade; information on Apatéon's crimes. On their return, Adélaïde's lover bared his soul to his father. Rosin, surprised by the embarassment with which Valincourt expressed himself on the subject of Adélaïde, wrested half his secret from him: he couldn't stop from feeling at the bottom of his heart a secret joy, & hope.

When they returned, Fanchette was gone, she had accompanied Agathe to her mother's house. (And this was the day, dear readers, when the publisher of this veritable story saw Fanchette at the fashion merchant's boutique, & when her pretty little foot was, for him, the divine Clio.[27] They were preparing that beautiful girl's adornment for the following day; the girl who called out to Fanchette at that time was the young Agathe; the man who was caressing her was Satinbourg.) Rosin could no longer live without her: he flew there with his son. On seeing her so beautiful, his heart throbbed with pleasure. "Ah! my son!" he said in a soft voice to Valincourt, that there is the object that should charm you: must Lussanville take her away from you!?" The young man, surprised, responded with a sigh: "Enough with the unfortunate man bit! you must ensure that my cousin is happy. As for me, I love someone else, as you well know: My father! I have bared my heart to you: everything depends on you." "How's that!?" "Who else but my father could ensure my happiness?" Rosin finally understood, & all his plans vanished into thin air. "You will

---

[27] Clio: the Muse of history.

be happy, my children," he cried out. And at that very moment, Lussanville, whom Fanchette had begged to find out more about Néné, came to tell her that he & his men were still unable to discover anything more about her.

Fanchette, on hearing this, could not hold back the tears. "O, what a price sensibility & tender gratitude place on beauty!" she thought to herself. Rosin said this to himself: "My how she would have loved her mother!" Lusannville thought this: "My how she will love her husband!" Nothing would console her though. But they did what they could to find the governess who, wherever she was, was attending only to the interests of her dear Florangis, whom her lover, her uncle, & Valincourt all escorted back to the convent.

On seeing the beautiful Adélaïde again, who came out to receive Fanchette, Rosin's antipathy for Lussanville was diminished. He would have been flattered by the double alliance, if it weren't for their odious mother's crime. Because, according to his principles, Adélaïde's misfortune was negligible, & his son's consternation was child's play: but the thought of Madame Lussanville made him shiver with horror. Nonetheless, touched by the friendship that the young man showed him, pressured by the desire to ensure his niece's happiness, to give his son a totally beautiful wife, & so rich a one as he then learned that the young nun was, he signed, even if with some repugnance, Fanchette's marriage contract, which the notary had just brought in. The good girl showed him just how touched she was by his goodness. He sighed: he was ceding two women who had charmed him: so much generosity didn't go unrewarded.

All three of them, after having left their two young friends, exited the convent; the day was done, the deserted roads around the monastery were covered in darkness: two women, who were walking rather quickly & with a frightened attitude, passed very close by. One of them bumped right into Lussanville, whom she hadn't seen: Fanchette's lover had barely opened his mouth, to excuse himself, when the young person threw her arms around his neck, & cried out: "Ah! my brother!" Lussanville, & Valincourt as well, froze, as they recognized Bibi's voice, whom Lolote was accompanying.

"It's not possible!" "My brother!" "Who would have thought!" "A perfidious..." "You're alive!" "... abusing my confidence..." "Apatéon!" "Who else? He persuaded me to pretend I had died of smallpox, & when he took off with my mother, he had me abducted." "What did you expect, good God!" "To be reunited with Valincourt: he tricked me, the traitor! he was thinking only of himself: but the wicked man got nothing from it: buried alive, my despair alone sustained me. Today, I don't know by what stroke of luck, I found myself abandoned by an old jailer, whom he had set watch over me: I was waiting for him in vain until evening: I thought I was going to die of famine. I rattled the door of my prison: & I was surprised to find it unlocked: I exited; no one was there, nothing stopped me: outside, I saw this young person, & I begged her to conduct me to my sister's convent."

My readers can imagine what an effect this astonishing recitation must have had on Lussanville & Valincourt. They accompany Bibi back to the convent, with Lolote, whom Lussanville was happy to see again. Adélaïde's & Fanchette's surprise was beyond words. Joy followed: Bibi found two loving sisters. This young person, making the sign of the cross, looked even lovelier: & Rosin thought to himself: "finally, this one has no lover; she will be mine." Nevertheless, he was not ignorant of what had happened: but one has to understand that he esteemed virtue & beauty, & not chimeras: this was yet another reason for his offering his hand in marriage to Bibi. He trembled: then all of a sudden the idea of his sister's death put a cap on his joy. Lussanville, for his part, thought about acquitting himself with Lolote: he offered to pay her pension at the convent, in the event she wished to stay there, & to set her up one day.

But the moment when everyone has nothing more to be desired draws near. The curtain will fall, & already the villain is punished.

Last Chapter

Happier than one thinks.

Three days had passed since Fanchette's triumph with the magistrate at the courthouse. They passed just as we have seen; & they were employed in preparations for the marriage of Fanchette to Lussanville; to prepare for Adélaïde's leaving the convent; to grow anxious, to search one's soul, to find oneself again, to recognize each other; to love, to say it out loud, to repeat it a thousand times that they would love each other forever & ever; to caress Agathe, to hear her vaunting her happiness; to ask Bibi a thousand questions, to console her, while promising her a husband; & one hundred other things that it would be too tedious & take too long to mention.

Finally the fourth day arrived (the day of the desired union) & Lussanville, Rosin, & Valincourt, followed by a numerous procession, presented themselves at the convent door. The Mother Superior escorted Fanchette richly adorned, beaming like the sun, & more fetching, more beautiful than a brilliant. She hands her over to her groom, who embraces her. The lovable young man spent several moments enjoying this delicious occasion. Finally, turning towards the nun, he said: "Madame, that's not everyone: I entreat you to read this" (a bailiff presented the order) "& to free my sister. I leave here at your house all she brought with her at the time she entered: I want her only." The Mother Superior could not get over her surprise: she asked for some time to deliberate with the elders: Lussanville was pressed for time; he added, that this very day, he would cause to have remitted to the Mother Superior a fund of 1000 *livres* of pension that the sister could enjoy. She considered it; the offer of a pension could go a long way with her good girls; she decides that Adélaïde can leave immediately. When one went to tell her, she had already put on again the clothes of her original station in life. The nuns accompany her to the door: Bibi follows her: they embrace: they exit. And there are no words to express Rosin's joy, when he pressed Bibi's pretty hand.

They had just arrived at the kind Florangis' uncle's house, whence they were going to present themselves at the foot of the altar: Fanchette asked about her nanny, & expressed the most fervid anxiety, when the sound of a carriage could be heard in the courtyard; it was Monsieur Apatéon's: they saw Néné get out of it: "Let's go, kids," she said to the lovable Florangis, Lussanville, Rosin, whom she recognized, whom she embraced, but whom she didn't have time to interrogate: "Let's go; there is no time to lose: come witness the last instants of a miserable man whom remorse has decimated." And immediately she makes them understand that the old Apatéon had sent men to go find her: that she had been unable to see him without being brought to tears. "He's wounded, children," she added: "the villains whom he had allied with to persecute you, & whom he wanted to vindicate at your expense, punished him: the Count d'A*** & he reproached each other before the magistrate: on exiting, the count & the Marquis de C*** ganged up on the old man, who was too fond of his body to have ever fought before, & who refused to draw his sword: those two miserable men, not satisfied by beating him with a cane, had the cowardice to draw their swords on a man who begged for his life on his knees. The guilty men were stopped; it took a great deal of effort to pull them away from him. I spent the night consoling the moribund: he reproaches himself for his awful crimes, which he wants to confess to you: Let's run, my dear child: I think he plans to leave his entire fortune to you: he's asking for you...." The lovely Florangis caressed her nanny: at that moment in time, she was only aware of the pleasure of seeing her again. Then she felt pity for Apatéon's lot; she shed tears over her vile persecutor. O virtue of tender hearts, precious sensibility, sweet prerogative of an enchanting sex, the one tear you shed is worth more than heroes' victories!... Lussanville & Valincourt themselves were moved: Rosin, whom his son had informed of the devout man's infamies, blessed Heaven for having exacted vengeance, offers his hand to Bibi with a satisfied look on his face: they all depart, they fly, they arrive.

What a spectacle, great God! a dying man presents, whose life was a fabric of horrors! who has not even, in order to assure himself against a terrible future, the sad benefit of incredulity! whose conscience presents to himself the memories only of young girls having been forced, deceived, seduced, bound, abandoned; innocents oppressed, & all his crimes! The discouragement, the fright, the despair torment him more than his illness even: he suffers from infinite ills. Such was Apatéon at this moment.

"Approach, Fanchette," he said, in a faint voice, "O you whom I have so offended, much more than you even know... What! Adélaïde! & her sister! Rosin! I am eternally grateful to the Supreme Being that you are all here: my confusion will be the greater for it... but will it equal my infamies? Fanchette, & you yourself, Lussanville, come here. My dear children, I asked you here to beg your pardon. You will shudder. But observe my suffering, my remorse, & my tears: & if some day vice should present itself to your eyes under a seductive shape, remember my fateful day. I used to be virtuous, as long as a wise father watched over me in my early years. I lost him. Well! would that I had followed him to the grave! False friends, pernicious counsels corrupted me: in a few years time I had surpassed my masters. But as I had always maintained a disciplined exterior, I hadn't visibly changed: I impressed people; I was thus admitted into honest families, where I brought my disorder & my corruption. How many girls were precipitated into crime & ruin under their mother's very eyes! abducted, kept in houses that my riches permitted me to possess! As long as I was young, inconstant, & flighty, I hardly kept the same mistress for long: at that time those poor souls passed into others' hands, & often from there, to the last degrees of vice, into awful prostitution. However, Heaven did not always allow me to sully innocence; I ran aground with you, Adélaïde, for instance; you thought yourself, falsely, the victim of my brutality; you were troubled, you lost control over your lost feelings; having recovered, you thought you had been vilified. Nothing happened: believe me, although I was indignant at that terrible moment; the truth alone remains."

And Valincourt, releasing a cry of joy, knelt before his lover, upon whom earlier he had not dared lift his eyes. "I adored you & I respected you, my dear Adélaïde," he said to her: "but when you called me your spouse, I noticed you grew red in the face..."

"Get up, you imbecile!" interrupted Rosin: "don't you realize you are uttering stupidities?"

"Beautiful & virtuous Florangis," continued Apatéon, "you, who for a time believed me your protector, listen, this will horrify you: it was I who, unable to make your mother listen to me, gave anonymous tips to Monsieur de Lussanville, whom I thought was my rival, & I combatted him without peril, not to mention that I was the poor devil who hounded him, & that I had come out on top. I didn't stop there; I was responsible for both your parents' demise, trying to pressure your mother to give herself to me physically. I didn't succeed; enraged, I shortened her days, & knew how to redirect suspicion onto Madame de Lussanville." "O, you monster!" cried out Rosin & Lussanville! And that kind girl, in Néné's arms, broke down into tears. Valincourt looked at Adélaïde, sighing. "That's not all," Apatéon resumed: "I had myself introduced to Madame de Lussanville; I recognized the young Rosin; I resolved to ruin him adroitly; & I would have easily succeeded if the virtuous magistrate, before whom we appeared, hadn't been as good as I was malicious. I wanted to seduce Adélaïde; I abducted Bibi; unpityingly, I saw their mother die of regret for having caused the unhappiness of one of her daughters, & lost the other. O Fanchette! the awful crime that remains for me to confess was in vain: I abused your trust, my power, your youth, your happy innocence: Heaven protected your virtue as if by a miracle; Néné was its instrument. Never forget that grace. To repair my crimes, as much as I am able, I want to leave to you all that I possess: accept, I don't say a gift, but a more than due restitution for what I caused you to lose." "Yes, Monsieur," responded Néné, overjoyed to see Fanchette richer than Lussanville himself now, "she will take it. Ah! I see clearly that you are good at heart, that it is your evil companions who corrupted you." It's in this way that a generous gesture captures the souls of simple & upright folk. Apatéon sobbed: "But who will bring back her father, whom I took from her, when her nascent charms excited criminal desires in me!"

The angel of death seemed to be waiting in the wings for the confession of this last infamy before striking its victim: a weakness overcame the vile man, whereupon he expired; but less miserable clearly than he merited. Everyone was seized with horror. "Who would have thought!" Néné cried out. Rosin went & hugged Lussanville & confessed his unjust hatred of him, which had subsided, based on feelings that Bibi inspired in him: the same day was chosen for their union as that of Valincourt's with Adélaïde: they all dried Fanchette's tears & left for the altar.

Finally the marriage knot was tied, & hymen was attained, whose virtuous love stoked the flame:

sacred vows united Fanchette & Lussanville: this charming girl gave to him what so many men had so many times before tried to steal. Several days later Adélaïde married her lover, & Bibi was united with Rosin in holy matrimony. They shared in equal portions the financier's succession; Apatéon's fortune went to Fanchette, who received also a considerable gift from her uncle. The young Agathe & her husband were not forgotten; Monsieur & Madame Lussanville gave them some of Apatéon's property: a rare example of generosity over the course of many centuries, when everyone normally just keeps what he has! Monsieur Kathégètes, touched by Néné's behavior, wanted to remove from her the opprobrium of being an old maid, & offered her his hand in marriage: everyone was basking in joy.[28] And it is in this way that love & wealth join forces to reward virtue.

---

[28] Original footnote: Fanchette looked after Lolote, who, receptive to the her kind benefactress' lessons, loves all the virtues she sees her practicing.

www.ingramcontent.com/pod-product-compliance
Lightning Source LLC
Chambersburg PA
CBHW030738110726
47900CB00008B/2351